A Light in the Storm

A Light in the Storm

a novel

CHRIS HEIMERDINGER

Covenant Communications, Inc.

Covenant

Cover painting by Todd Purser

Cover and book design © 2000 by Covenant Communications, Inc.

Published by Covenant Communications, Inc.
American Fork, Utah

Printed in the United States of America
First Printing: October 2000

07 06 05 04 03 02 01 00   10 9 8 7 6 5 4 3 2 1

ISBN 1-57734-684-X

Library of Congress Cataloging-in-Publication Data

Heimerdinger, Chris.
    A light in the storm : a novel / Chris Heimerdinger.
        p.   cm.
    ISBN -1-57734-684-X
    1. Traveling sales personnel--Fiction. 2. Married men--Fiction. 3. Blizzards--Fiction. 4. Fathers--Fiction. I. Title.

    PS3558.E454 L54 2000
    813'.54--dc21   00-043054

For Beth

My pulse, my light, my vision
Into the eternities

Prologue

THURSDAY, DECEMBER 24

Christmas Eve

I have a story to tell.

A story for the winds. A story for the mountains towering over me like dark-robed priests on a death-watch. A story for the starless night sky above my snowy grave. And for the angel whose beacon of light has just appeared from beyond the horizon—come, I assume, to guide me to my eternal destiny. But not a story that I will ever tell to living souls.

Oh, how I wish I could have told it to my children, my precious ones, wide-eyed with innocence and brimming over with unconditional love. I wish I could have told it to Jillian, my sacred gem who loved me for so long despite the loneliness and heartache burning in her breast. It might have lessened their pain, brought closure to the mystery of what had become of me. And perhaps revealed the truth of how much I really loved them.

But I've lost all hope of that now. All hope that I'll ever tell my story to anyone in this life. I can no longer feel my limbs. They're like lead weights. Like lifeless, bloodless branches on a dying tree. The flesh of my face is also numb, deadened by the bludgeoning winds. I can see the drifts of crystalline whiteness pressing against my broken body. I see it all by the light of the approaching angel. The snows blow over me like a burial shroud as I lay on the summit of this isolated mountain. In minutes my face will be covered over entirely, and everything will become silent at last.

All I can do in these final brief moments is mourn. I grieve for so many misguided choices and warped priorities. Mostly, I mourn that the one chance I might have had to redeem myself was so cruelly denied. I've experienced the most extraordinary events, the most breathtaking visions. But the secrets of these will die with me too. This is the most painful fact of all. To know the truth. To see the light. And to have no opportunity to make a difference.

I wonder how often it is in the history of humankind that God grants to men or women in their final moments of life, when they are powerless to report it, a vision as all-encompassing and penetrating as mine. I suppose it happens more often than anyone would believe. The inability to report it may even be part of the punishment. The first torment of other torments to come.

But I'm too weak, too full of pain, to contemplate the ramifications of that. With all the energy left within me, as the tunnel of light overtakes my soul, I'll recount the marvelous story of what I've seen, of what has befallen me since that fateful day two weeks ago.

I'll recount the events in my mind. I'll utter them from the depths of my darkening consciousness. And perhaps some entity of eternity—perhaps this angel whose beacon flies toward me from the realms of heaven—will carry some semblance of its message to the hearts of those I loved most in this world. It's not much to ask. And the message is so simple. Just to let them know how sorry I am. And how, if I had lived, I would have done everything in my power to make it right. *If I had lived* . . . It sounds so empty now. But it's all I have left to hope.

So listen, Angel. Listen to me, O descending Light. I've only a short time left. Only a few precious moments before my consciousness passes from this world to the next. And there's so much to tell.

So very much to tell . . .

Day 1

Three days.

My husband would be home in three days. Then I had a decision to make. A decision that would affect the rest of my life.

The question I kept asking myself was, did I still love him? I wasn't sure I wanted to know the answer. I was afraid of it. Because despite what I felt, it might not have been enough. Sometimes all the love in the world can't change anything. It can't change another person's heart. That's what I'd been trying to do for fourteen years. I'd been trying to make my husband into something he wasn't. I'd been lying to myself. It was time to face the truth.

For the last five years I'd practically raised my three children by myself. Zackary was twelve now. Tamara was ten, and little Corban was eight. They hardly knew their father anymore. Corban hardly knew him at all. He was just that busy, ill-tempered man who came home some weekends and spent most of the time in his office downstairs. Ben had missed so many years. So many ball games, piano recitals, and Sacrament meetings where he could simply sit at our sides. At first I'd tried to be patient and supportive. A new business, after all, requires a certain amount of sacrifice. I guess I just didn't expect to have to sacrifice everything. And to sacrifice for so long. Now Ben was expanding his company beyond even his own expectations. I had to face reality. Things weren't going to change. He was living his own dreams, his own obsessions. And the rest of us were not really included.

Maybe I wasn't strong enough. Maybe, as Ben had often told me, I should have been more grateful. But the luxuries he was promising couldn't fill the void in my heart. They couldn't give me what I felt was most important—the blessings of an eternal family, one day reunited in the presence of God.

A few days after Thanksgiving I'd given my husband an ultimatum. I'd told him he had to make a choice—either his family or his business. I could tell he was upset. But he said nothing in response. And then he made his choice. An hour later he left for Montana on a two-week sales tour without acknowledging a word I had said.

That was eleven days ago. He'd be home Monday night. I had three days to make up my mind. Three days to decide what was right for my children, and for my own peace of mind. I had no idea what I was going to do. No idea what was right.

The answers would come, I told myself. But I was starting to realize they weren't going to come through anxiety and fear. They had to come from God. Please, I *prayed*—let them come from God.

* * *

I was going home.

Never before had the full significance of that phrase hit me so deeply. I'd focused all my time and energy on other things for so long, it might have been easy to forget what those words meant. But I hadn't forgotten. No, this time it was going to be different. I'd had ten long days to think things through. It was time to start fixing the things I had broken.

I finished up my last appointment in Billings, Montana, around six-thirty. Then I spent the last hours of the evening shopping. Christmas shopping. For the last twelve years I'd left all the Christmas shopping up to my wife. This year I was determined to make it the best Christmas ever. There were nine presents in the various bundles and sacks under my arms as I made my way through the Rimrock Mall in downtown Billings—three for each of my children. The hour was late. The steel-grated barriers were starting to come down over each of the store fronts. I walked more swiftly. I still had one more present to buy.

My final stop was a jewelry store near the east exit doors. The clerk noticed me staring through the glass counter at a shimmering sapphire necklace with a silver setting that was shaped like a dove.

"Would you like to see it?" he inquired.

"Yes, I would."

After he handed it to me, I turned the stone in my hand to better catch the reflection of the lights. "It's beautiful," I said. "She likes sapphires. She always has."

"You have wonderful taste, sir."

"A dove means peace—am I right? A fresh start."

"Yes, sir. I believe it does."

I smiled. "Perfect. I'll take it."

"Excellent."

"Box it, wrap it. I have to get on the road."

"Long journey?"

"Salt Lake City."

He raised an eyebrow. "That *is* long. Are you going to try and make it all the way tonight?"

"As far as I can."

I carried all my presents to the parking lot and stacked them on the floor of my cab-over camper—all but the necklace I'd bought for Jillian. That one I took with me inside the cab. Before I started the engine, I stared at the little gold box in my palm. Was I being a fool? Could a little jeweled trinket really make up for so much pain? So many cruel words? Could the damage ever really be repaired? I carefully tucked the package in the glove box. I had to believe—I had to hope—it was still possible.

The dashboard clock read 10:00 P.M. I grabbed some fast food at a local drive-thru and started heading out of town. The skies above I-90 west of Billings were spangled with a million stars. They looked so close I might have reached out and scattered them like fireflies. Normally at this time of night I'd have found a cheap motel and called it a day. But not tonight. I'd finished my sales tour three days sooner than expected. With any luck I'd be home Saturday afternoon, three days early. I hoped it would be a pleasant surprise. My family needed some pleasant surprises.

I knew I'd pushed Jillian to the edge. For the last five years she'd practically been a single parent. Five years ago I'd bought into a line of health-care products developed by a chemist from the Goshute reservation of western Utah. *"All the natural secrets of the ancient Native Americans."* That was the hook I'd used. My ointments and balms and herbal supplements were now sold in over two hundred different outlets throughout the western states.

The enterprise had kept me on the road for weeks at a time. Jillian did well for the first few years. Finally the sacrifice got to be too much, the hours too long. At Thanksgiving I'd told her I'd found an investor who would take our products nationwide. The announcement was meant to inspire celebration. Instead, it got me an ultimatum. My family or my business. At first, I was infuriated. Did she think I *enjoyed* working so hard? Didn't she realize that I was doing it all for her and the children? I'd left that evening without speaking another word. Just walked out the door. But there was nothing I could do about it now. Water under the bridge. I only hoped I hadn't burned my bridge to the ground.

I turned south at Laurel, Montana, and hooked up with Highway 212 to Red Lodge. I knew these roads well. I'd grown up in these parts. A hundred or so miles south lay the tiny metropolis of Cody, Wyoming. Cody was the town of my boyhood, the place where I'd forged half of my memories and all of my dreams.

A lot had changed since then. Progress had spoiled many a vista. Much had changed about me as well. Back then I'd wanted to build rocket ships to the stars. My earliest years were ingrained in my memory like a fairy-tale on the other side of the fog. Even today, at forty-one years old, I sometimes had the impression that half my life took place before I was seven. I remember adventures and camping trips. I remember Christmases with glittering trees and laughter and presents so deep you could swim in them. But all that changed one snowy November night.

When I was seven years old, my father died.

Yes, yes, I know. I wasn't the first kid to ever lose his father. People should just get over such things and move on. And honestly, I felt I *had* gotten over it. But as time went on, I came to realize how Dad's death affected me not only with a terrible grief, but with a terrible drive— a yearning to leave behind a legacy that was much more enduring than the one that my father had left us.

After the car accident on South Fork Road that took my father's life, my mother was left with six children and the family business, a twelve-room motel on the West Cody Strip. Dad had also left a mountain of debts. Within two years the bank had repossessed the motel, and my mother was waiting tables at Cooley's Cafe.

Mom's tips were never enough to feed seven mouths. She was too proud to ask for welfare—even from the LDS Church. We helped out however we could with odd jobs and chores: mowing lawns, shoveling walks, collecting pop bottles and tin cans. Some weeks this made up our entire grocery budget. Our clothes were always worn to the very last threads—an embarrassment that we endured whenever we set our feet on the playground. Determination had welled up inside me from a young age that I would never live that way again. I'd find that pot of gold—no matter how long it took and no matter what I had to sacrifice.

Now I was beginning to wonder—perhaps I'd had that pot of gold all along. It seemed ironic that my ambitions were nearly costing me everything that was supposed to be the most precious—my eternal family. To be honest, I wasn't sure I hadn't lost them already. Soon I would know. Obviously another "sorry" wasn't going to be enough this time. But maybe a *thousand* sorrys and a sapphire necklace would be a good beginning.

Only the day before, I'd even taken the first steps to fulfilling my wife's ultimatum. I'd called my investor to ask if he'd be interested in buying the business outright. He was flying in from California on Monday morning to meet with me and my sales manager, Ed Gallagher. If everything went the way I expected, I'd finally be able to give my family all the time and attention they required.

Finally. As the highway rolled beneath my wheels, I contemplated that word for a long time. For some reason it sounded far more empty than I would have expected. Considering how much I'd lost, how much I'd missed, I wondered if achieving that nebulous state called "finally" really made any difference at all.

I took a last drink from the Dr Pepper I'd ordered with my beef and cheddar sandwich. Then I found the cherry turnover I'd ordered for dessert. One bite convinced me I could never get it down. The thing was hard as a rock. I rolled down the window, tossed it, and then watched in the rearview mirror as the pastry made two high bounces and rolled into a ditch.

As I peered out at the darkened hills, not a speck of snow reflected in the moonlight. The slopes were as brown and pine green as they had been in August. It had been an unusually mild season—and right on the heels of one of the worst winters on record. Usually to get home at this time of year I'd have to take I-90 to

Butte, or state roads to Rock Springs, Wyoming. The route I hoped to drive tonight was far more scenic, and by coincidence, several hours shorter. My goal was to reach Cooke City, Montana, at the northeast gate of Yellowstone National Park by two or three A.M. Then, if my body insisted, I'd pull off onto the shoulder, climb inside my cab-over camper, and steal a few hours of slumber before heading out again. Just enough that I might still catch the first rays of the rising sun on the gnarled peaks of the Absaroka Range.

I pulled into the old mining town of Red Lodge and found an Amoco station at the south end of town. After topping off both of my fuel tanks, I stepped inside to pay the attendant, a wiry-looking man in a greasy *Seattle Mariners* baseball cap.

"Is the Beartooth Highway still open?" I inquired.

"Far as I know," he replied. "Hasn't been more than a whiff of snow all season."

I smiled in satisfaction. The sixty-four-mile stretch of Highway 212 between Red Lodge and Cooke City usually closed around mid-October. A good portion of the road was completely above timberline, rising to an altitude of almost eleven thousand feet. With snow so scarce, the U.S. Forest Service must have decided there was no reason to lock the gates.

"Wouldn't surprise me if it stays open through Christmas," the attendant added. "That'd be one for the record books."

I thanked him and climbed back into my pickup. I realized I might even be home for lunch. It seemed a shame to be crossing the Beartooths in the dead of night. Charles Kuralt, the old news anchor from *CBS*

This Morning, had once dubbed it "the most scenic highway in America." Or so it said on several posted road signs. This remote highway held a lot of memories for me. I'd driven over it in my very first car shortly after I got out of high school. It was at Beartooth Lake, on the other side of the pass, that I'd caught my very first fish on the last camping trip that I'd ever taken with my father.

Just beyond Red Lodge, my pickup began its ascent. The thick shadows of the pine trees whisked by shark-swift on either side of the pavement. A few miles further on, the road began its first nail-biting switchback. The curve was a little sharper than I remembered. The last time I'd driven it was in a '72 Chevy Impala. Now I was in a '95 Ford F-150 with a bulky cab-over camper. I wondered about my merchandise in back. Hopefully, my last remaining boxes of ointments and balms wouldn't topple over and damage the newly wrapped presents. I took the turn slowly, resolving to put the gifts in the closet beside the kitchenette the next time I stopped.

As I continued winding up the switchbacks, the awesome Rock Creek gorge stretched out below me like the jaws of a dragon. The sheer cliffs, painted silver by the moon, looked almost other-worldly, like something God had left undone. Nevertheless, the steep overlooks did little to curb my impatience. I continued to take the turns at ten or so miles above the posted speed limit of 15 and 25 miles per hour.

It wasn't long before I reached the top of the east wall and bypassed a sign welcoming me to "Wonderful Wyoming." The hardest part of the trek was behind me.

From here it was an easy overland cruise across the granite tundra until the steady descent carried me back into Montana, finally reaching the tiny tourist hub of Cooke City.

I took a deep, gratified breath. This part of the highway was almost always buried under ten feet of snow about now. Every few yards along the roadside a long stick impaled the earth—guides for snowmobilers who crossed the Beartooths in the dead of winter. A hearty lot considering the biting temperatures and ceaseless winds. But for now, the entire stick was exposed. The roads were clear. And uncharacteristically quiet. I realized that I hadn't passed another vehicle since just out of Red Lodge.

The dashboard clock now read 12:00 midnight. I fought down a hard yawn and shook myself, forcing my eyes wider. The goal was still to reach Yellowstone by 2:00 A.M. To insure alertness, I switched the air conditioner to cold. Then I spun the dial on the radio, trying to find a station without any static. No luck. Ever since I'd broken off the antenna in a car wash, reception had been poor. I gave up and faced forward. The divider lines passed steadily beneath my headlights. The effect was hypnotizing. My thoughts started to drift.

About the time I reached the sign announcing the summit of Beartooth Pass—Elevation 10,947 feet—my eyelids fell shut. I swear they were only closed for a second or two, but when my chin snapped up, my front tires were headed for disaster. I jerked the wheel and centered myself, barely escaping a collision with the guard rail. I heaved a sigh of relief. It might be best, I decided, to stop for a couple of minutes. Just to walk around in the brisk air, maybe check the merchandise in my camper.

But as I searched for a place to pull over, a strange sight flashed in my headlights. There was a man standing on the right side of the road. I drew my eyebrows together. A hitchhiker? At this hour? In the middle of nowhere?

The man had an old frayed army-green backpack draped over his shoulder. He was dressed in a heavy brown parka with a thick fur lining around the hood. I'd never been much inclined to pick up hitchhikers—no matter what the place or season. But at this unholy hour, he seemed far more likely to be someone in trouble. And yet, thumb up, his expression was calm, as if Beartooth Pass were no different than any freeway on-ramp.

Curiosity had the best of me. I pressed on the brake and rolled slowly to a stop beside him. The hooded face leaned forward, peering into the cab. He seemed as curious about me as I was about him. A glint of light caught his weathered features. An eerie feeling flooded up my spine. The man's expression seemed—how can I describe it? Approving? Grateful? I'd almost call it *satisfied*, as if he'd been awaiting my arrival for a very long time.

I reached over and unlocked the door. He pulled it open and climbed inside. He was not the young fool I might have expected. Instead, he was an older fool, mid-to-late fifties. A drifter, I imagined. Someone who might hitchhike as soon as ride the rails. Under the dome light his eyes looked almost luminescent, as piercing as the sapphire in Jillian's new necklace.

"What are you *doing* out here?" I asked, my tone suggesting he might be crazy.

"Same as you," he replied good-naturedly, shifting his travel pack onto his lap. "Just drifting from one place to another."

He shut the door. The dome light extinguished, preventing me from scrutinizing his features any further. I wished I could have studied his face a moment longer. I was just about to draw a comparison with a face I'd seen before—some fuzzy image from an old movie or a nineteenth-century photograph. But as soon as the light snuffed out, I lost the connection. It was the strangest thing. Only a few seconds had passed and my memory of the drifter's features had already faded.

I pressed on the gas and continued down the highway. "Where are you headed?" I inquired.

"A place I've never been," he replied. "But it's the place I should have been headed all along. I guess I got distracted."

"Where would that be?"

"Home," he replied.

"Ah," I said, then I thought to myself, *He's a philosopher.* "I know what it's like to get distracted from that. So where's home?"

"Same place you're going."

I shifted in my seat, feeling a little bit conned. Obviously, to this old drifter, "home" was anywhere he could hitch a free ride. I didn't much like the implications. I wasn't sure I wanted a perfect stranger sitting shotgun with me all the way to Utah. "I can take you as far as Cooke City," I said. "Then I'll have to drop you off."

I knew Cooke City had motels, maybe even a bus depot. He'd find everything he needed. I could drop him off with a clear conscience. Then I'd drive on into the Park, find a scenic overlook, pull off the road, and snooze.

The old man sighed. "I was hoping we could go a little farther, but . . . you're the driver."

I wanted to change the subject. My next inclination was to ask for his name. It was only natural. Certainly expected. But for some reason, I wasn't all that interested in knowing. I felt oddly uncomfortable and I wasn't sure why. All at once I felt I'd be happier if the two of us said nothing at all for the next thirty-five miles.

It was the stranger who stoked a conversation. "Cold night."

I realized I still had the air conditioner set on cold. I switched it back to heat. "Yup," I agreed. "Pretty warm for this time of year, though."

"The forecast says it will snow."

"Does it? I haven't heard. I don't care much for the radio. Even when it gets good reception."

"It's definitely going to snow."

I gave him a curious glance. His face remained only dimly illuminated by the cobalt green glow of the dash lights. How could he be so certain, I wondered? Where would he have heard such a forecast?

"I suppose it can snow all it wants," I said. "Nothing much can slow down this hummer." I slapped the dash of my pickup. "But if you ask me, this is gonna be one brown Christmas."

"Are you ready for it?"

I drew my eyebrows together, trying to decide what he meant. "Ready for what?"

"Christmas."

"Oh. Ready as ever, I guess. I'm not sure if it's ready for me, but . . ." I let the statement trail off, not anxious to burden him with my personal problems. I tried to turn the conversation. "What about you? Are you ready for Christmas?"

He turned it back again. "I'm more curious about you. Let me ask you a question—"

Haven't you asked enough already? I thought.

"If this were your last Christmas, who would you spend it with?"

"Spend it with? My family, I guess. Isn't that what anybody would say?"

"Is that what *you* would say?"

I'd figured it out now. This was a game. I needed more details. "Why is it my last Christmas?"

"Some things we don't have any choice about. Other things . . . our choices might even save our life."

I scrunched my forehead. Could this have come any more out of left field?

"The choice is yours," he repeated. "You can spend it with anyone."

I gazed off into the headlight beams. "Anyone, eh? Well, now, if my choice is *anyone*, I'd have to think about it. I guess I'd—" I turned to look at the drifter again.

The seat was empty.

A wrenching gasp clawed at my throat as I slammed on the brakes. The pickup started to skid. I yanked at the wheel and fought to regain control. The tires threw up gravel as they slipped off the left side of the pavement. At last I brought myself to a lurching halt. The truck and camper sat askance in the middle of the lonely mountain highway, the engine idling, my thoughts raging. Again I looked at the passenger seat.

The drifter was gone.

I sat there hyperventilating, my heart pumping like a locomotive. The world outside was graveyard quiet. The granite plateau might as well have been an isolated pass in the Himalayas. I gripped the steering wheel and strained to steady my mind, reorient my bearings. *No way*, I told myself. This couldn't have happened. Drifters with backpacks couldn't just vanish into thin air.

I focused into the headlight beams again, squinting. Just up the road, bright and legible, stood the sign that read: *Beartooth Pass, Elevation 10,947 feet.*

"But I passed that sign," I muttered. "I passed it back—"

Suddenly it hit me: that sign was the last thing I remembered before dozing off at the wheel. A dream, I wondered? It was so *real!* And yet . . . what else could it have been?

"Wow," I sighed from the depths of my lungs.

Without a doubt it was time to pull over and get some sleep. But how could I be expected to sleep now? My mind was racing a million miles per hour. I wondered if I'd ever felt so awake. Every detail, every word of the dream blazed in my head like neon. The only part that remained a little fuzzy was . . . well, the man's face. This should have been evidence enough that the whole thing was a dream. And yet every other detail was so crisp, so vivid. If I doubted this, I might as well have doubted every memory in my brain.

The thudding of my heart relaxed to a normal rhythm. My breathing started to steady. I laughed out loud. Unbelievable. Somewhere in my subconscious lurked an imagination that I didn't know I had.

I straightened the wheel and pressed gingerly on the gas pedal. The truck rolled forward. I tried to put the dream out of my mind, crush it out like a hot ember from a campfire.

Shortly, the road began another series of jagged winds and turns. Pockets of scrubby pine trees popped up now and then, evidence that the road had started its descent. I passed several elaborate icicle formations at the roadside where springs had frozen into the cliff face. These were the only visible evidences of winter. I tried to be careful taking the curves near such formations, realizing that water might have frozen over the pavement. And yet the full breadth of the ice sheet at one particular corner eluded me. Before I knew it, my wheels began slipping out from underneath the chassis.

The forward momentum of the pickup transformed, almost gracefully, into a 180-degree spin. The "whoooaa" in my throat elevated into a full-pitched yell. The back end of the truck twisted off the right side of the road. The rear wheels dropped. My stomach leaped into my mouth. The fear of death knotted in my chest. Just how deep was the ravine on my right? Then came the crunch. The pickup became stationary. Dreadfully stationary. I sat still for a moment. Finally, I shuddered with gratitude. No harm done. I pressed my foot on the gas. The Ford made a feeble attempt to wrench free, then the tires began to spin. I was stuck.

"Oh, please," I groaned. "Don't do this! *Not now!*"

I threw open the cab door. I didn't even have a flashlight. Only a tiny penlight on my key chain. But as it turned out, this was all I needed to make the grim diagnosis. Looking under the truck, I saw a sharp boulder under the rear axle. The vehicle was hopelessly high-centered. Even four-wheel drive wasn't going to pull me out of this one.

At least the truck was still fairly level. The embankment only sank about three feet, then rose up again, dropping off into a wide gorge nine or ten yards further down. I hadn't even been close to falling over any edge.

"Well," I mumbled. "I'm stuck. Stuck for the night."

It'd take a tow rope and winch to pull me off that boulder. The nearest wrecker was likely in Cooke City, still twenty or thirty miles away. I peered off into the gloom, wondering anxiously when the first car might make its appearance. Since I hadn't seen another vehicle since midnight, it seemed probable that no one would come along much before daybreak.

Might as well get some sleep, I decided. I could keep one ear tuned to the highway. But considering that my hood projected halfway out across the right lane, another driver would likely stop to investigate without much prompting. I switched off the headlights. Then I made my way around back and unlocked the camper.

Before stepping inside, I took another breath of lung-biting air. The silhouettes of the mountain peaks loomed all around, giving me the impression of a council in judgment. I felt an odd sense of reproach. A whistle of wind moaned up there somewhere. A lonely sound. Mournful.

Suddenly another sound cut through the night. The two tones had blended perfectly for the first few seconds. Finally, the second sound distinguished itself.

It was a howl.

I'd never heard the howl of a wolf before. At least that's what I assumed it was. I'd read somewhere that wolves had been reintroduced into the wilds of Yellowstone back in the early 90s. Some of the creatures had apparently migrated into the Beartooths. The sound was completely unexpected . . . and a touch unsettling.

I took the last step into my camper. Just as I leaned out to shut the door behind me, the first flake of snow melted on my cheek.

SATURDAY, DECEMBER 12

Day 2

"*Mom, when are we going to get a Christmas tree?*" *asked Tamara.*

My daughter had always been overly excited about Christmas fanfare. If it was up to her, we'd start decorating in mid-September and leave it up until Mother's Day.

"*Maybe we should wait until your father gets home,*" *I said.*

"*How come?*" *asked Corban.* "*Let's get a tree today and have it waiting for him when he gets here.*"

"*I'd just prefer to wait,*" *I said.*

My tone was a little more stern than I'd intended. The fact was, I really wasn't certain where we would be spending Christmas, but I didn't feel prepared to explain this to them.

"*What's the matter, Mom?*" *asked Zackary insightfully.* "*We're gonna have a tree this year . . . aren't we?*"

It felt like my heart was being squeezed with both hands. "*How would you feel about spending Christmas in Phoenix with Grandma and Grandpa?*"

"Would the cousins be there?" asked Corban.

"Maybe."

"They drive me crazy," he declared. *"I don't want to spend Christmas in Phoenix. I want to spend it here."*

"Why would we go to Phoenix?" asked Tamara. *"Grandma and Grandpa usually come* here.*"*

"It's . . . it's just an idea."

"Would Dad be there?" asked Zackary.

The car went silent as the children waited for my reply.

"I think he might have to work," I said.

There were no more questions. My children understood far more than I wanted to admit.

* * *

When I awakened, I was shivering terribly. Only as I stirred to full consciousness did I realize that I'd actually been cold for some time. I'd been fighting to remain asleep in spite of it. I focused up at the curtained window inside the sleeping nook. It was light outside. And yet the quality of the light did not reflect the brightness of a mountain morning. It was subdued somehow. By clouds or . . .

I reached up and slid back the curtain.

"Holy Moses!"

It was snowing! Not just snowing. A *blizzard!* A whiteout!

I hit my head on the roof of the nook. Cursing, I rubbed the bump and threw off my Indian blanket. I stumbled down into the main compartment and flung open the door. Immediately my face was stung by a blast of icy wind.

The transformation took my breath away. The evergreens along the slope of the gorge were blanched white, like a column of skeletons. I could only see about twenty yards down the highway in either direction. The road was *gone!*—totally invisible under three or four inches of blowing snow.

"What *happened?*"

I couldn't have slept more than four or five hours. How could the world have changed so dramatically in so short a time? It seemed *instantaneous!*

Panic boiled inside me. The cab. I had to reach the cab of the pickup. Gritting my teeth, I shielded my face under one arm and plunged into the tempest, staggering and leaning into the wind. It seemed an incredible distance to the front of the truck. I reached the driver's-side door and dug my hand into my pocket to find the keys. I could hardly see through the blowing flakes. I fumbled to stick the key into the lock. I cursed myself. Why had I even bothered to lock it? What was I afraid of? Car thieves? Out *here?* If a thief could have pulled me off that rock, I'd have *given* him the darn truck!

I finally pulled it open and sprang onto the front seat. Forcefully, I yanked the door closed, shutting out the chaos. Then I sat there, eyes closed, listening to the thump of my heart. At last I shook the snow from my hair. I turned the key in the ignition. The engine coughed and started. I whipped the heat levers to their warmest setting. Frozen air rushed from the vents. Impulsively, I grabbed a book of matches from the ashtray, half-tempted to strike one to warm my fingers. I thought better of it and tucked them into my shirt pocket. I tried the windshield wipers. The blades hesitated, then slapped into action. Thankfully they hadn't frozen to the glass. I rubbed my hands together. They continued trembling, but not just from the cold. The seriousness of my situation crashed down on me like a grand piano.

"No cars are coming today," I mumbled. "There's no way."

I tried to chuckle out loud to relieve the tension. It didn't work. I breathed deeply. I was stuck here for the day. There was no getting around it. Someone would come as soon as the snow let up. No doubt it was standard procedure to send a truck or a snowplow over the pass before officially closing the road. Tourists and fools like myself must have gotten stuck up here every year.

But how long would the storm last? The way it looked, it could last all day. Maybe into tomorrow. My body tensed with frustration. I pounded my fist on the steering wheel. The horn let out a short honk, carried off quickly by the storm.

So much for any plans to surprise my family. What a miserable stroke of luck! I'd *needed* those three extra days! Needed them to convince my wife that I'd had a change of heart.

"This can't be happening!"

Be calm, I told myself. My family would still be there tomorrow. I looked at the gas gauge. There was still over three-fourths in the first tank and a full barrel in the second. So that was one bit of good fortune. I could warm up the cab as often as I needed.

I considered food and water.

As far as water, Mother Nature had provided an ample supply of that. I could fill a container with snow whenever I desired, then leave it in the cup holder next to the heat vent to melt. I reached under the seat and found my 32-ounce plastic Big Sipper cup. I dumped in the block of leftover ice from last night's Dr Pepper and manipulated the heat vent to hit it directly. *No problem*, I thought. Water was going to be no problem.

Now for food.

"Food . . . not so good," I admitted.

I glanced at the floor and saw the shiny foil that had once wrapped my beef and cheddar sandwich. In the past I'd often saved a portion for later. But not this time. I'd snarfed down the whole blasted thing.

I reached under my seat again. It was a habit of mine to always keep a bag of chocolate bridge mix under there. I pulled out the empty plastic envelope.

"That's right," I remembered deflatedly. "Finished it Thursday."

Was there food in the camper? I didn't think so. Even the vitamins from my product line had been sold out at my last stop in Billings.

"So be it," I gruffed.

I'd been hungry before. Probably be hungry again. I grabbed the spare tire at my waist. There was a good twenty pounds of extra lard hanging there anyway. A day of forced dieting might even do me some good.

The air in the vent started blowing a degree or two warmer. I congratulated myself that I'd at least brought plenty of warm clothing, including a heavy winter coat. I'd even packed the wool sweater that Jillian had bought me on our last anniversary. As well as five changes of shirts, pants, and underwear. Plenty, I thought. More than enough.

But I couldn't fool myself long. "What a mess," I mumbled. "What a miserable, unholy mess."

Scenic route! Of all the asinine ideas. It was *December* for crying out loud! Who in their right mind would try to drive across Beartooth Pass in the middle of December! Obviously no one else had been quite as stupid. My truck had been the only vehicle on the road last night. Why hadn't anybody mentioned that a storm was coming? Like that wiry-looking attendant at the Amoco station. Wouldn't he have known?

And yet . . .

It occurred to me that the storm hadn't come as a complete surprise. I'd heard about it somewhere. Where was it? The answer startled me.

The hitchhiker.

The drifter's declaration still echoed: *It's definitely going to snow.* I sat back in wonder. My conversation with this apparition was still so eerily vivid. Had any dream ever stayed with me this long? I must have had dreams every night of my life, yet even if I strained my memory, I could only recall four or five.

Maybe it was more than a dream, I speculated. A premonition. A foreshadowing. Something more than a dream and less than reality.

I scolded myself. I'd never been the recipient of heavenly manifestations, and I very much doubted I was going to start now. Visions and revelations were for other people. People who *needed* such things. I'd never needed them. I'd always been able to lift and carry myself through every situation without bothering God.

Besides, I didn't feel I was worthy of such things. Of course, I'd been a member of the LDS faith for most of my life—baptized at eight, ordained at twelve, even married in the temple at twenty-seven. But I'd made a lot of mistakes in my youth. I could only claim to have been regularly active the first few years after I was married. It wasn't that I didn't believe. I felt sure it was all true, but . . . a man has to be *practical* sometimes. And when my business started to take off . . . Well, weekends turned out to be the best times to get caught up. As well as the best times to travel.

Hey, I *admired* those people who could devote all their lives and energies to the Church. I sincerely hoped that one day I could do the same. But for right now—just for a little while longer—I really needed to make sure my business stayed on track. Maybe if I'd had a normal nine-to-five job, it would have been different. Most people just don't understand what it takes to be successful—I mean *really* successful. After all, it's the twenty-first century! The world is rushing by so fast it's almost a blur. To compete, sacrifices are frequently unavoidable. And yet I felt my attitude was better than most. Because I was sure it was only temporary. Soon, time would become an unlimited commodity for me. But not quite yet. Only a few more months.

So I didn't give much credence to the drifter's words. In fact, the whole thing seemed almost laughable. If the heavens had sent me a dream about a drifter with an army-green backpack who could forecast the weather, well—it was proof that someone up there had an incurable sense of humor.

I sighed. Such thoughts were a waste of energy. What did it matter if it was a revelation or a dream or a drive-in movie? It didn't change my situation. I was stranded on the Beartooth Highway—four hundred miles from my family in the middle of a Wyoming blizzard.

I looked again at the bridge-mix bag. There were several stray crumbs of chocolate at the bottom. I poured the crumbs into my palm and licked it clean. As I savored the flavor, I stared out gloomily at the storm. It was going to be a long day. A very long day.

SUNDAY, DECEMBER 13

Day 3

"Mom?" asked my youngest son. "What does divorce mean?"

I looked at my son, then I looked away, trying to sound casual as I asked, "Who told you that word?"

"Zackary and Tamara," said Corban.

I should have guessed. Since I'd procrastinated discussing it with my children, it appeared they were taking the liberty of discussing it among themselves.

"What did Zack and Tamara say?"

"They said you and Dad were probably getting one. They said we'd have to move away and that you and Dad would hate each other and we'd never see Dad again." His eyes were moist.

"Oh, honey." I wrapped my arms around his shoulders and pulled him beside me on the couch. "Something like that wouldn't mean your Dad and I would hate each other and it certainly wouldn't mean that we would never see him again."

"Would it mean we'd have to move away?"

I looked away again. "I don't know, Corban."

"Then it's true. You are *getting a divorce."*

"I don't know that either, honey. Your brother and sister are just talking. But whatever happens, Corban, I want you to know that I would always love you. Your father too. Neither of us would ever leave you."

"What about Zack and Tamara? Zack says if you get divorced, some of us might live with Dad and some might live with you."

I felt a shuddering in my soul. I held my son a little closer. "I wouldn't let that happen." My voice cracked with uncertainty. "Everything will be just fine."

"Can we call Dad tonight?"

"I'm not sure how to reach him," I said. "He's still on the road."

"Do you think he'll call us?*"*

"Maybe. I hope so. But even if he doesn't, he'll be home tomorrow night. What did . . . what did you want to say to him?"

"I just wanted to tell him I love him."

Tears pricked at my own eyes. To Corban it didn't matter. He loved his father, no matter what. His daddy was the sun, moon, and stars. A part of me wished my son could remain innocent forever. Another part of me envied him.

"I'm sure he'd like to hear that," I said. "I'm sure you can tell him tomorrow night."

"I love you too, Mom."

I laid his head back against my neck. "Thank you, Corban. I needed to hear that too."

* * *

I flung open every cabinet and cupboard, drawer and closet, one by one. My actions made no sense. I *knew* there was no food in the camper. I knew it with every strand of logic in my brain. But I didn't care about logic. I pushed aside all the empty boxes. I stripped off every cushion and dug my hand into every nook and cranny in hopes of finding the smallest morsel, the tiniest crumb. A forgotten can of vegetables. A half-eaten Oreo cookie. *Anything* to stop the gnawing in my stomach. Hunger had given me the most restless, ungratifying night's sleep of my life.

The search took less than five minutes, producing nothing. I leaned against the wall to settle my nerves. I couldn't remember the last time I'd gone a whole day without food. Not since I was ten years old. Not since my sister had forced me to go on a twenty-four-hour fast. She said it would clear my head, open my spirit to God. All I remembered was feeling miserable. The next day I ate three full-course meals in one sitting.

I shook my head in disgust. This was ridiculous. It had only been one day. What kind of man was I? I wasn't dying. Just hungry. I was fine.

"Get a grip, Wylie," I told myself. "Get back to the cab."

Since my camper had no propane, the cab was the only source of heat. That is, other than the heat I tried to generate under four layers of clothing. I went to the camper door, hesitating before opening it. Just as I feared, it did not fall open under its own weight. I had to push.

The sight wrenched at my stomach. The snow was now three inches higher than the base of the door. It was over *three feet deep!* The blizzard continued raging all around. Any shred of hope that I'd be rescued today was carried off by another gust of wind.

Clenching my fists, I leaped into the snow and forged a new trail to the front of the truck, raising my knees high. My pant cuff slid up. The snow fused to my shins, burning like fire. The drifts had blown against the base of the driver's-side door. I yanked it open. To escape the white sea, I practically had to dive onto the seat, carrying a heap of snow with me inside the cab. I shut the door and brushed it off my pants, off the seat, and onto the floor. Two inches now filled the floor space! There was no escaping the stuff!

I turned the ignition. The engine fired right up. Thank Heavenly Father, I thought, for whatever device the engineers at Ford had installed to keep my battery alive. Again the vents blasted my face with frigid air. I was shivering uncontrollably. I tried to warm my fingers with the heat of my own breath, and made another half-hearted effort to find a radio station. The story was the same as yesterday.

"Static? Static? Is that all you can say to me, piece of junk?!"

I punched the dashboard. What was the problem!? I was ten thousand feet above sea level, for crying out loud! My radio should have at least picked up *something*, shouldn't it?

I tried the wiper blades. Frozen solid. Too much snow had piled on the hood. My only porthole to the outside world was a clear circle on the passenger-side window, on the lee side of the blizzard. Even that was disappearing inch by inch as the snow swirled around it and froze to the glass.

I have to clear the hood, I thought.

"Later," I mumbled. "Later, later, later."

As life-giving heat began to fill the cab, my nerves started to steady. My mind settled into a controlled, sober depression.

My investor would fly in from L.A. in just a few hours. Ed would be driving down from Boise. Tonight they'd both try to call me from their hotels, eager to confirm the details of tomorrow's meeting. And where would I be? Not one step closer. Not three feet from this exact same spot.

They'd first call my office phone downstairs. Jillian never answered that phone. She'd let the machine get it. If only she'd answer it, then she'd know that I'd been heading home early. She'd know something was wrong. It would never happen. That phone could ring until doomsday.

No one would realize I was missing until tomorrow morning. And then just Ed and my investor. Ed had come to expect this kind of thing from me. I often came home a day or two late from road trips. Mr. Jager, however, was a different story. He'd likely be furious. After all, I was the one who'd called the meeting. Even after I was rescued and could explain the whole story, my opportunity to sell him the business might be in serious jeopardy. All my plans to obtain financial security and meet Jillian's ultimatum might be in jeopardy. I shuddered in frustration.

It occurred to me that Jillian had also come to expect me home a day or two late. I recalled a time or two that I'd actually forgotten to call and tell her. My own family might not consider me overdue for a week!

Somehow I felt if I wasn't home by tomorrow evening, my wife and children would not be there when I arrived. I felt another surge of panic. Just as I was ready to make a noteworthy change in my life! Jillian would never believe my story. She'd need photographs, eyewitnesses, fingerprints, and blood tests. Even if she *did* believe me, what would it change? I'd used up all my second chances.

I reached over to the glove box and pulled out the brightly wrapped package containing the sapphire necklace in the setting like a dove. As I turned it over in my hands, thinking of my fragile, neglected wife, it occurred to me that this was just another version of the same tactic I'd used so many times before. I'd often bought my family nice gifts to make up for my failings to them in other areas. Suddenly I began to look at that silly necklace like a hangman's noose—a noose I'd created with my own hands. If I gave it to her under the present circumstances, it might only seal my fate.

I realized it might be some time before anyone decided that I was really missing. It could be weeks. It might be never.

I shook myself. Never mind. I was letting my imagination get away from me. I'd be out of here as soon as this lousy storm let up. Everything was going to be just fine.

I rolled down the window and scooped some snow off the side mirror into my Big Sipper cup. Then I set it back in the plastic holder to melt.

"Tomorrow," I mumbled.

Tomorrow the rescuers would come.

"Tomorrow I'll devour an entire pepperoni-and-pineapple pizza followed by an entire chocolate cheesecake smothered in raspberry syrup and washed down by a barrel of the sweetest, coldest . . . "

I paused. Better not to think about food. For some reason, such thoughts made me terribly thirsty. And it took the snow in my cup far too long to melt.

MONDAY, DECEMBER 14

Day 4

"Mom," asked Zackary. "Can we put lights in the backyard too?"

I laughed. "Why would you want Christmas lights in the backyard?"

"'Cause it's cool," Zack said simply. "Our neighbors over the fence would see them."

"Fine," I said. "If there're any to spare."

I'd relented on my pledge not to buy a Christmas tree. As soon as the kids got out of school, we went and bought the fattest, roundest Norwegian spruce on the lot, as well as a half-dozen new strings of lights to festoon around it. The kids had been going gangbusters ever since, not even stopping to eat dinner. All they could think about was decorating the house and yard as bright and colorful as possible before their father got home. It was as if they believed that somehow the magic of Christmas might heal and cure and make right all that was wrong.

I must confess, something inside me wanted to believe it too. Despite the gloom that had been hanging over me all *day long, I couldn't help but feel a sense of courage and well-being. Perhaps it was the glow of the lights, the faith of my children, or maybe the spirit of Christmas itself that convinced me I might leave the door of my heart open just a crack. Just enough that I might allow him to speak the first word. I felt I'd know in two seconds, just by the look in his eyes, if my hopes were vain, if there was a chance that we might ever build something eternal together. If that look wasn't there, I told myself I would never look for it again.*

I realized it was getting dark.

"Come in now, kids," I said. "I've made soup and breadbowls. You have to eat before bed."

"But Mom," Tamara protested, "we want to stay up for Dad."

"There's no telling how late he'll be home," I said. "It's a school night. I promise I'll leave the Christmas lights on until he arrives."

"Will you wake us up?" asked Corban.

"If it's not too late."

"Promise?"

I made the Boy Scout sign.

After the children had gone to bed, I waited up in the living room, watching the lights blinking across the front yard. I waited for those familiar headlights to turn into the driveway. With each passing hour, my heart sank deeper into the cavity of my chest. It was very late before I accepted the truth. He wasn't coming. Once again, Ben Wylie had failed to keep his word. I felt like such a fool.

The door of my heart closed for the final time.

* * *

I sat unmoving in the silence, peering through the tiny hole in the passenger-side window, memorizing the contours of the ice-glazed ridge. The snow continued to fall. Three days' worth of snow. Someone had pulled the cork out of heaven. At least the wind had died somewhat. The snow now fell in massive floating flakes, like tufts of cotton. It was nearly five feet deep. Five feet in three days.

I fought off another wave of claustrophobia. The walls of snow seemed to be closing in. *How long could it keep snowing!? Could I be buried alive?* I pressed a trembling palm to my forehead, trying to relieve an escalating headache brought on, I assumed, by a lack of food. I was ready to admit it now. I was freaking out. Definitely freaking out.

"I've got to get out of here," I announced to the stillness.

I had to get home. Somehow I had to reach my family. But what could I do? Hiking out was out of the question. I'd be lost in the drifts. And yet I had to do *something. What could I do?!*

The first fuel tank was empty. I'd started into the second. I realized I'd have to use the heater more sparingly. Earlier I'd made an effort to clear the snow from around the exhaust pipe to avoid asphyxiating myself. I was so weak. The effort had nearly killed me. I could still feel the strain in my muscles. I'd also dragged my blankets and the rest of my warm clothes into the cab. This was where I'd decided to wait out the rest of my ordeal. It was just too cold in the camper. Besides, walking back and forth through the drifts required too much energy.

The emptiness in my stomach now felt like the twisting blade of a knife. How many days, I wondered, could a human being survive without food? I was sure I'd been taught at one time or another. I just couldn't remember. The wrapper from my beef-and-cheddar sandwich caught my eye again. I snatched it up. Carefully, I uncrumpled the foil. Against the inner layer I found a patch of dried, orange-ish cheese. I scraped it off and chewed it to bits, spitting the piece of foil that tore off with the cheese onto the floor.

Then I sat there morosely. The hunger still burned. I thought again about the cherry turnover I'd tossed out the window. Had I really tossed it away? Something compelled me to believe I hadn't really done it. I'd stuffed it under the seat, stuck it in the glove box. I examined both places for the tenth time, even pulling all the letters and bills out of the glove box to prove the point once and for all. No. I'd really done it. I'd really thrown it to the birds and beetles.

I lay back on the seat, still pressing my forehead, not bothering to clean up the letters and bills. The corner of one envelope folded up in front of my eye. Irritated, I pulled it out from behind my head. I was about to toss it onto the floor when the return address caught my attention. It was from my son, Corban. The postmark was from last May. He'd mailed it to my hotel in Dallas. The letter was open, but I only had a faint memory of reading it. I pulled out the folded square of paper and read it again.

Dear Dad,

    I hope you get this letter. Mom says it should reach you just in time before you leave.

I just wanted to tell you that my story won first place over everyone in the whole second grade. It's about a dragon named Arthur who takes me on a ride to the moon and Mars and Pluto. This Friday I'm going to read it in an assembly in front of the whole school. I was hoping you could come and hear it. It starts at 2:30, but I might not start reading until 2:45 in case you can't come before that. It would be so great if you could come. It's the last day of school. Afterwards, I'll even take you out for ice cream at Baskin Robbins. I got money helping Mrs. Jeppson in her garden, so I'll even pay.

Even if you don't have time for ice cream, I'd still love it if you come see me read. I promise I'll do a really good job.

Love,
Corban

I read the letter again. I read it a third time. I shook my head. Why couldn't I remember reading it last May? I must have skimmed it, stuffed it in the glove box, and forgotten it entirely. As I recalled, I'd gone to Dallas to supervise the manufacture of one of our products. A mistake in the labeling had put the whole thing behind four or five days. That Friday must have come and gone. Corban never said a thing. Never even asked where I had been.

My heart started to ache. I found myself leafing through the other letters on the seat. I found another one. It was from Jillian. It had been sent to my hotel in Las Vegas during the convention last August. Amazingly, it hadn't been opened at all. I must have figured I'd get to it later. But I never did.

I took a deep breath and tore it open.

Dear Ben,
This is a difficult letter for me to
write. I wanted to write because it seems
like whenever we talk in person, all we
do is fight. I need to get out all the
feelings in my heart, so please bear with
me.
   First, I want to tell you I love you,
Ben. Your happiness has always been the
most important thing to me. I've tried to
support you in everything you do. But I'm
starting to realize it's not enough. I need
support, too. I have my own dreams. I've
tried to sit down and tell you about
them several times, but something always
comes up. I feel like I'm sinking, Ben.
Sinking into despair. I've never been so
lonely in all my life. I need to start
doing some things for myself and for the
family and I need your support as much
as you've ever needed support from me.
   I know how much your business means
to you. I know how hard you've worked.
But lately I feel it's only been tearing us
apart. Is it really worth sacrificing every
thing else in your life? Zackary skipped
school the other day with his friends. I
tried to talk to him, but I couldn't make
any headway and it just turned into a
shouting match. Every day he seems to be
growing more distant. Tamara was crying
the other night. When I asked her why,

she said it was because she had a night-mare that you'd been in a car accident and were never coming home. Do you have any idea how that made me feel?

I never wanted a bigger house, Ben. I never wanted riches. We need you. The children need you. And I need you.

I really want this marriage to work. But I can't do it alone anymore. Please think about what I've said. Please reevaluate the things that are most important. I've set up an appointment with a marriage counselor on the 28th, the week after you get back. It's at 4:30 P.M. at Jordan Valley. Please put it in your calendar.

I hope everything is going well in Las Vegas. We look forward to seeing you when you get home.

Love,
Jillian

I sat there in a daze. My heart felt as if it had been stabbed through the center. An unopened letter from my own wife. How could I have forgotten it? I did remember soon after I got home from the convention her mentioning something about an appointment with a counselor. I'd replied that it wasn't a good time—she should have checked with me first. I remembered the look of devastation in her eyes. As usual, I told her she was overreacting. We didn't need a counselor. What she needed was a *prescription*—one of those popular antidepressants. Then I went down to my office.

The pain in my heart deepened. How could I have been so callous, so blind for so long? Suddenly all my arrogant hopes for winning back my family seemed like the most pathetic scheme I'd ever devised. I'd destroyed her, slowly but surely. I'd crushed my children. My hopes had been a fantasy from the beginning, a pipe dream. I'd lost my family. I'd lost my Jillian. Lost her forever in the haze of my ambitions.

And for the first time it occurred to me. It was exactly what I deserved.

TUESDAY, DECEMBER 15

Day 5

The phone rang at about a quarter to nine.

"Hello, Jillian?"

The voice sounded urgent. I recognized it immediately. It was my husband's sales manager from Idaho. The line, however, sounded local.

"It's Ed Gallagher. Is Ben there by any chance? I've been calling his office all weekend. All I get is that dang machine."

"He's not here at the moment."

"Do you know when he'll be back?"

"We expected him home last night, but apparently he didn't make it."

"Really?"

"No. Is there something wrong?"

"Well, it's just that he called me on Friday and said he'd be home Saturday afternoon. He missed an important meeting yesterday. The client is flying back to California in an hour."

"He told you he'd be home Saturday?"

"That's what I understood. Did he tell you where he's staying?"

"No," I said, somewhat embarrassed. *"He stays in so many motels. It's hard to keep up with him."*

"Did he ever get a cell phone?"

"Not yet. New Year's resolution, I think."

"I see. Sorry to have bothered you. I know he doesn't like me to call this number. When you hear from him, tell him to call me, okay? I'll be back in Boise this afternoon."

"I'll tell him, Ed."

"Thanks, Jill. I appreciate it."

"Ed?"

"Yes?"

"If you hear from him first, could you . . . have him call us?"

I think Ed heard the quaver in my voice.

"I will, Jill. I promise. Thanks again."

After I'd hung up the phone, I stared off into space. A cold feeling crept into my chest. I wasn't sure if it was anger or something else. Was it fear? No. The scene was too familiar. He'd be home tonight. No doubt about it. The question was, would I be home to greet him . . . ?

* * *

"It wants your soul. The lupus. It wants your soul."

I'd fallen asleep in the cab sometime around noon. The voice—the voice in my mind, in my dream—caused me to stir. It was a whispered voice, like the sound of something rustling in the leaves. A kind of reverberation seemed to linger even after I opened my eyes. I was sure that the voice repeated the phrase a third time just as I was coming to: *The lupus wants your soul.*

"Lupus?" I repeated dreamily. My flesh felt prickly, as if something unearthly had just entered and departed my frame.

What the heck was a lupus?

That is, besides a terrible disease that had contributed to the death of my oldest sister back in the late seventies? Something told me that the word had another meaning. *It'll come to me*, I thought. But then I wondered if I wanted it to. For reasons I didn't understand, the word had frightened me to the very core.

I tried to sit up. The blood rushed to my head. I had to pause, leaning on one elbow. I felt weak. Drained. The feelings of hunger in my stomach had subsided into a low, throbbing ache, but at least there were no more noises. It had been nearly five days since I'd eaten a solid meal. Unbelievable. But here I was. Breathing. Functioning. Thinking. Well, sort of thinking. My thoughts were becoming . . . strange. Hard to keep up with. Muddled.

As soon as the dizziness left me, I pushed myself up the rest of the way. Through the tiny porthole in the passenger-side window, I saw a sight that thrilled my soul.

"Sun!"

A single blazing ray shone through the porthole, magnified and amplified by the crystallized ice. The storm was over. It had been four days of uninterrupted whiteout. The glistening shelf of snow stretched out in every direction, sometimes rising higher than the level of my eyes, resting against three sides of the pickup.

I pressed my face against the glass to feel the sunlight. Oh, it felt good! The nightmare was almost over. The nauseating hunger. The exhausting boredom. The endless days and nights. Almost over. There was no bad weather to hinder them now. My rescuers could arrive at any moment.

Suddenly a gasp escaped from my throat. The truck was virtually buried. They'd never see it!

"I have to clear the roof!" I declared. "In case they send a plane. Yes. They'll send a plane."

Another wave of nausea twisted in my stomach. Where would I find the strength?

"I'll find it," I muttered. "I have to."

Then again, I thought, maybe my rescuers would arrive by snowmobile. Yes, that made more sense. There were too many nooks and crannies along the length of the highway—too many places where a plane might miss a snowbound vehicle. I felt I'd gotten stuck in just such a cranny. A steep incline arose on the left side of the road. If a plane flew behind that ridge, it might miss me entirely.

That's it. They'll send a snowmobile. Likely they'll send a half-dozen snowmobiles!

But the anxiety wouldn't let me go. I had to clear the hood and roof. Despite my lack of energy. Despite everything.

I pushed open the passenger-side door. I'd given up trying to open the driver's-side door. The snow had drifted over the top of the truck on that side. I'd made it a habit to open the passenger's side at least four or five times a day to keep from getting trapped.

My joints felt enervated, as if the sinews that held my bones together might disintegrate, leaving my body as limp as a rag doll. My legs plunged into the drift. It felt just like plunging into a frozen lake. For some reason, all the layers of clothes against my skin weren't enough to keep me warm.

My eyes scanned the distance from the hood of the truck to the roof of the camper. Three feet of snow had piled on both surfaces. How could I ever clear it? The broom. The only tool I could think of for snow removal was a broom in the camper.

The prospect of getting inside that camper seemed just as overwhelming as pushing off the snow. Any trails I'd forged to the camper door had been reburied by snow and wind, erasing all evidence of my labors the day before. So much energy—wasted. Once again I began plowing the snow with my arms, throwing myself forward like an animal caught in quicksand. It seemed an eternity before I finally pulled myself onto the floor of my camper.

Sleep, I thought. Now all I wanted to do was sleep.

"This is enough. Enough for today. Today I cleared the doorway. Tomorrow the roof."

Suddenly I heard a sound in my mind—an engine roar. The roar of an airplane. The sound was only in my imagination, but it forced my eyes wide open. I couldn't wait! I had to clear it *now!*

I struggled to my feet and found the broom closet—the same closet where I'd packed all the Christmas presents I'd bought for my family that first night. The broom handle stuck up through the middle of the brightly wrapped gifts. I yanked it out. It was a small broom with flimsy, plastic whiskers. It would have to do.

I stumbled back outside and forced my brain into a trance, running scenes from my favorite movies through my mind. Westerns mostly, with Clint Eastwood and Sterling Weymouth. I'd mutter the dialogue like a lunatic. I became stuck on the line, "Idiot. It's for you," from *The Good, the Bad, and the Ugly.* All the while as my plastic-whiskered broom pushed snow from the roof and hood, I muttered the words, "Idiot. It's for you."

My knees buckled. I nearly blacked out, grabbing one of the side mirrors of the truck and hanging there like Sterling Weymouth clinging to the roof of a fast-moving locomotive.

When my balance recovered, I forged ahead. Soon I made a discovery that withered my heart. The bottom layer of snow—the layer that sat directly against the metal of the truck—had frozen into an inch of solid ice. Fighting back my emotions, I started chipping away at the ice with the opposite end of the broom. The truck was bluish silver—exactly the color of the snow when the sun hit it just right.

"How 'bout this cherry red Chevy 4x4?" the salesman at the dealership had asked.

"Too much," I said. *"The price is highway robbery."*

"Suit yourself," he replied. *"That's as low as I can go."*

So I went with the silver-blue Ford in his competitor's car lot across the street. Another of life's uninspired decisions.

The sun was just setting behind the western peaks as the last chip of ice fell away from the hood. I leaned on the broom and took in my work. All at once the reddening sky started spinning. I tensed my muscles to ward off the second spell of dizziness. It didn't work. My thoughts blanked out, just like a television screen cut off by an electrical outage. The feeling terrified me, like sinking into a cauldron of blackness.

It was the growl that snapped me back to reality.

I stood there for a moment, leaning against the door, wondering if the noise was somehow part of another dream. But then I heard it again, and the sound made my flesh crawl.

I raised my eyes. There, on a ledge about thirty feet up the opposite embankment, staring down at me like a slavering demon, it stood. A wolf. Not just a wolf. A monstrously sized wolf with a sleek, raven-black coat and piercing yellow eyes. The hair on its neck stood needle-stiff and its nostrils steamed in the frozen air. Its lips curled back to reveal a set of ivory-colored fangs.

I was gripped by recognition. I *knew* this creature. I'd known it all of my life. I'd felt it in the dark. I'd seen it slinking in the alleys and I'd heard its footsteps in my wake. I'd seen those eyes in my nightmares and, on occasion, staring back at me from the mirror. This animal wasn't driven by hunger. It had only one objective. To see me destroyed. I knew this without explanation. Knew it with my whole soul.

My heart was seized by terror. I dropped the broom, ripped open the cab door and threw myself onto the seat, nearly catching my own leg as I slammed it shut. Had the wolf leaped? I felt sure it had pounced the instant I had dropped the broom. I'd cleared just enough of the windshield to make out the obscured, distorted image of the ridge above my truck. I turned the ignition and flipped the heater to Defrost to try and give me a better view. But though I pressed my nose to the glass to try and see around the windshield's icy striations, there was no sign of the raven-black beast. Vanished. Evaporated. As if it had never been there in the first place.

Another hallucination? I was losing my mind! Hunger and boredom were driving me insane! And yet I was lucid enough to recall the definition of the word. It seemed to me that I'd first heard it in a horror movie about full moons and their powers of transformation.

Lupus was another word for wolf.

THURSDAY, DECEMBER 17

Day 7

"Mom, do you think people can talk to each other in dreams?" asked Tamara.

"What do you mean?"

"I mean, can they send messages—tell each other things—even though they're far away?"

"I don't know, Honey. What did you dream?"

"I dreamed about Dad. He was really cold. It was dark and he was scared."

She was genuinely upset. The entire household was upset, and for good reason. By Thursday it was a record. Ben had never been this late. He'd never gone this long without calling. I'd tried for three days to believe everything was fine. I'd been through this before. It was just another act of monumental thoughtlessness. Twice I'd gone so far as to pull my suitcases out of the closet. I'd even written down an itemized list of everything I would have to pack for the children. I just couldn't bring myself to do it.

It seemed a remarkable coincidence that last night the Bishop had showed up on my doorstep. Bishop Masservy was *several years younger than Ben. He was a kind man, a good leader, but he was also a man I'd known for many years. Perhaps it was for those reasons—his age, and because I knew some of his own faults and failings—that I'd never sought him out for counsel. But last night I'd swallowed my pride and opened my heart. He'd offered comfort and listened. Perhaps all I'd needed was someone who would listen.*

"What's the use?" I asked him. "If my husband and I can't build an eternal family here, *what chance is there that we'll have an eternal marriage up* there?"

"None," he agreed. "But you're only at halftime, and you committed—covenanted—to play the entire game."

It wasn't easy for me to hear, and a part of me had resented it. But another part—a wiser, more visceral part—had been aching to hear those words. He gave me a blessing and left. After that, I decided that before I made any decision about my marriage, I would confront my husband again.

That was yesterday. This morning I found that I was well beyond such thoughts. Something was terribly wrong. I just had no idea what to think. Had he been hurt? Did he have an accident? Had he been kidnapped? What was I supposed to think!?

I called Ed Gallagher for the fourth time. He still hadn't heard a word. Not since last Friday. If Ed was right, Ben should have been home Saturday afternoon. He'd been missing for nearly a week! Oh, Ben Wylie, *I moaned in my heart,* please let this be another thoughtless act. Please walk through that door tonight. If for no other reason, for the sake of the children.

"I have a bad feeling," my oldest son reported to me. "Something is wrong. I think Dad's in trouble."

"What are we going to do, Mom?" asked Corban.

"First of all, we're not going to panic," I said. *"Second, I think it's time that we called the police."*

* * *

"Ben."

I heard it. Or I thought I heard it. And my mind stirred from an uneasy sleep.

"Ben Wylie."

"I'm awake," I mumbled, dreaming that the voice was one of my older brothers, rousing me to start my morning chores.

"You haven't made your choice."

The voice was clear. But it was not my brother. My eyelids fluttered open. I looked toward the passenger side of the cab. Someone was sitting in the shadow created by the sheet of new snow on the windshield. I could see the silhouette of a man in a heavy brown parka with a thick fur collar.

I pinched my eyes tightly to try and restore focus, attempting to drive a sharp wedge between reality and the world of dreams. I heard an abrupt slam, like a car door. My eyelids shot up. I scrambled to pull myself upright on the seat, my heart pounding in my throat.

The figure was gone.

I tried to draw a breath. No air would go into my lungs. I wiped frantically at the fogged window to see out into the snow on the passenger side. Where was it? The ghost. The wraith. Where had it gone? There was nothing but the still drifts and the engulfing granite gorge.

I drew back, my thoughts caught in a whirlpool.

"It's happening! It's happening again!"

I was hallucinating. Two days ago it had been the wolf. Now it was the drifter, back again to repeat his incomprehensible message, back again to torment my mind.

It's because I'm starving to death, I told myself. It had been seven days without food. An entire week! This long without nourishment, I was bound to start hallucinating. I reached up shakily toward the rearview mirror and angled it toward my face. The sight turned my stomach. My skin was pale and chalky. My lips were cracked and chapped. My eyes were dead. Like steely black marbles pressed into the sockets of some carcass at the taxidermist. The extra twenty pounds that I'd accumulated over the last ten years was surely gone by now. From here on out, it would be all muscle that was disappearing. Ben Wylie himself would be disappearing.

I looked away, sickened and depressed. And yet I was lucid now. The visions couldn't hurt me.

But if I really believed that, why was I so frightened to leave the cab of my truck, even to refill the Big Sipper cup with snow or to relieve myself? It was because it was still there. The lupus. I knew it. I could feel its presence, lurking, circling like a predator around a wounded animal. Seeking my soul.

I believed in the wolf. The drifter might have been a hallucination. But I believed in the wolf. And yet there was no more reason to accept the reality of the wolf than the reality of the drifter. No wolf would ever hunt this high. There was no game. The snow was too deep. Wolves roamed in packs. The year they released wolves into Yellowstone I remembered seeing report after report trying to dispel the myth of the savage, man-eating wolf. One article even claimed that no wolf attack on humans had ever been reliably documented in all of American history.

But none of this mattered. Something in my primeval heart rejected such reports. It was the creature's demon eyes. I could still see them. The wolf was hunting me.

Through the crystallized glass on the passenger-side window I could see the brightness of the sun. And yet I dared not hope that today was the day. Yesterday the sky had been just as clear. The temperature had been warmer. And still, no one had come. I'd been forgotten. The world had forgotten that I even existed.

It was time to accept the truth.

"I'm dying," I announced to the emptiness.

Forty-one years of life were about to come to a grinding halt. Forty-one years and it would all end here. In the middle of the Beartooth wilderness. The middle of nowhere.

What mark, I wondered, had I left over the course of my life? What would they remember about me after I died? What would people say?

I could hear my Jillian even now: *"I feel sorry for him. He died alone. But that was the way he lived. Not really needing anyone. Not really loving anyone. Not even the people who loved him."*

I could hear my children: *"Sure, we miss him. Aren't kids supposed to miss their dad? Actually, we don't remember him all that well. He was always gone. Even when he was home, he was gone. We were sad for a while, but then things got back to normal."*

Tears welled up in my eyes. What legacy had I left? How had I changed the world? What causes had I fought for? What wrongs had I righted?

Few.

And then I confessed: *None.*

"So what!" I resounded to heaven.

The primary struggle of my entire life had been survival. From the time my father died when I was seven years old, I'd worked like a dog.

"Like a *dog!*" I declared.

"Your choice, Ben . . ."

I stiffened, eyes wide. I'd heard it right in the middle of my ranting! I looked around in desperation, trying to pinpoint the source. It was as if the voice had spoken right behind my ear. Behind *both* ears! No, no, this was impossible. I was lucid now. I couldn't hallucinate when I was lucid. I started reciting a list of facts. My name, address, and phone number. The first sixteen presidents. The list of products in my catalogue. Anything to prove to myself that I was not going mad.

My eyes fell on the radio.

The radio! Of course!

My fingers sprang to the dials. *Yes!* It was on! Just a half turn was enough to prove that it had been on all along. Crackling static coughed from the speakers. I'd left it on from earlier that morning when I'd gone through my usual routine of trying to find a station.

It was the radio! It wasn't a hallucination. Just some freak of nature and atmosphere.

As if to prove me right, a miracle happened. An announcer's voice suddenly rang out on the dial. Until now I'd only managed to catch a word or a phrase or a note of music, quickly drowned out by static. But this voice was crisp and clear!

"*. . . calling for light snow between now and midnight. Partly cloudy tomorrow and clearing up for the rest of the week. But look out for the weekend. Another storm may be headed our way. So don't put away your snow shovels just yet. It's 10:33 this Thursday morning. You're listening to KODI, Cody, Wyoming . . .*"

My heart melted. It was the station I'd grown up with. To hear another human voice—it sounded almost alien. And music! As the D.J. finished the weather report, the song "Thunder Rolls" by Garth Brooks took over the airwaves. I turned up the volume. I turned it up quite loud, almost ear-splitting, as if the sound itself had the power to ward off any further hallucinations.

For the remainder of the morning, I basked in the sounds of my unexpected companionship. The radio was like a new friend. My closest friend.

"I'm not alone," I whispered. "The world goes on."

Around noon, static seeped back into the broadcast. Slowly it began to overtake the voices. The atmospheric disturbance that had created my unusual reception was dissipating.

It was about one o'clock that afternoon, as Reba Macintire crooned the lyric, "*I might have been born plain white trash, but Fancy was my name . . .*" that I became aware of a droning sound overhead.

At first it didn't register. The music was very loud and the sound had blended with the static.

"Oh no!"

I lunged toward the passenger door and pulled up on the handle. I fell outside into the fresh snow and shielded my eyes from the sun so I could gaze up at the sky. I could see it! An airplane!

"Heyyy!" I waved, my voice cracking. "Down here! Down here!"

But the twin-engine Cessna had already flown over me. It was headed away, into the sun.

I fought back a bout of coughing and shouted again, "Down here! Heyyyyy!"

The plane was disappearing behind the ridge.

I pulled myself upright, kneeling in the snow. My body and face were coated with flakes. "Pleeease! I'm here! I'm . . . down . . . here."

The plane was gone. If it was a search plane, I knew the search was over.

I fell face forward into the drift. Reba Macintire's voice inside the cab had disintegrated into pure static. I remained there in the snow, my face becoming numb. I debated if I should remain there, allowing the numbness to settle in for good.

That's when I heard the scrape of the claw against metal and ice. In dread I raised my eyes. It was poised on the hood of my truck. The sum of my fears. The bane of my aspirations. The creature's hungry, yellow eyes seared a brand onto my soul. As my eyes locked with those of the wolf, its lips curled back once again and a growl rumbled in its throat.

There was no escape. I could never reach the cab of the pickup. It had positioned itself for just this purpose. It seemed to know exactly what it was doing.

For the first time I became aware that the beast was not alone. A shadow moved at my right. Another animal let out a hellish bark behind me. I was surrounded. I couldn't count them. When I looked about, my eyes wouldn't focus. The wolves were like ghosts, moving lambently across the snow's outer crust, sending up clouds of snowy powder as they darted and turned. Partly in this world, partly in another. I knew that as soon as the leader lunged, the rest would be on top of me in seconds.

My veins filled with a warm rush of adrenaline. I gritted my teeth. Suddenly the monstrous black wolf leaped! I raised one arm for protection and used the other to grasp out for the wooden handle of the broom that I'd dropped two days before. The jaws clamped down on my forearm. My body was thrown back into the snow. The heat from its nostrils fanned my face. I had to protect my throat. But the wolf weighed as much as a lion! I could hear its comrades charging in. They were about to tear me apart!

Shrieking with rage, I thrust the broom handle toward the beast's face. The blunt end stabbed it right in the eye. There was a yelp. Its jaws released. My arm yanked away. Somehow I managed to find my feet and dive toward the open door of the cab. There were deafening snarls all around. In my peripheral vision, I saw several more animals in mid-leap. Just as my hand grasped the seat of my pickup, they landed. One clamped its jaws onto my coat collar. Another bit into the cuff of my pants. Even this close, the creatures looked watery, phantom-like. I saw only flashes of yellow eyes, claws, and flying fur.

With all the energy I could muster, I kicked and flailed and fought to pull myself inside the cab. They dragged me back to my knees, but I kept my fingers gripped to the base of the door. The black wolf recovered, more vicious than ever. It was about to throw itself back into the attack when I heaved my last leg inside the door and slammed it shut on another wolf's neck. I drove it back outside with a final kick into its snout and pulled the door closed.

That's the last thing I remember. I fell into a delirium almost immediately, lulled into unconsciousness by the static on the radio and the shrieks of the wolves outside. If I had incurred any wounds, I couldn't feel them. I vaguely perceived several places on my winter coat where the material had been torn and the white stuffing was hanging out. The multiple layers of clothing on my body had kept them from tearing my flesh. Nevertheless, I *had* been injured. Not by their jaws. But by the energy I'd exerted to survive. I had no energy to spare. When I finally awakened again, I couldn't be certain if one day had passed, or several.

SATURDAY, DECEMBER 19

Day 9

The young investigator, terminally polite and efficient, sat at my kitchen table thumbing through the various photo albums of our lives. He'd already selected two pictures of my husband that he felt would suit his purposes—one from a Christmas morning when Corban was an infant. Another from our wedding day at the Idaho Falls Temple, fourteen years before. It occurred to me that no recent picture of my husband even existed.

I'd asked my children to let me speak with the investigator alone; nevertheless I caught frequent peeks of them hovering about in adjoining rooms, straining to hear every word. They were sick with worry. Tamara hadn't slept for two nights. Corban seemed to cling to my side every possible moment.

I sat in the chair opposite the man, biting a fingernail. I felt terribly antsy and impatient. It had been forty-eight hours since I'd filed my initial missing person's report. I was irritated that it had taken this long for anyone to assign an investigator and that he was just now taking the initiative to gather evidence and information.

"So, Mrs. Wylie," he continued, "how many days would you say that your husband was away on business during a typical month?"

"Fifteen to twenty," I replied. "Sometimes more. It depended on the month."

"How often did he make this same swing through Idaho and Montana?"

"I don't know. Every three or four months, I guess."

"Did he always sleep at the same motels?"

"Not always. Sometimes he slept in his camper."

"And he told you he was coming home Monday night?"

"Yes," I said. "But he told Ed, his manager, that he would be home on Saturday."

The investigator looked at me keenly. "Did he often change his schedule without letting you know?"

"No, not very often."

"But it was known to happen?"

"Yes. Occasionally."

"Did he ever arrive home a few days late without calling or informing you?"

"Yes," I confessed.

"How many days was he typically late?"

"Just one or two. And he usually called. There's only been a couple occasions when . . . But he's never been this late. He'd have called by now. I know he would have."

"Mrs. Wylie," he said carefully, "how would you describe your relationship with your husband?"

"What do you mean?" I said, hedging.

"Did you two have any sort of argument before he left?"

"Yes, but . . . well . . . that wasn't really unusual."

"Can you describe the nature of the argument?"

"Well, we . . . " I started wringing my hands. " . . . I asked him to reevaluate his priorities. Devote less energy to his business and more to his family. The typical argument, I suppose, of many families—"

"How did he respond?"

"He . . . he walked out. We didn't really resolve anything."

"Did he ever threaten to end the marriage? Or did you threaten to end it yourself?"

I'd heard enough. "Listen, I know what you're thinking. But Ben wouldn't just leave without saying a word. Yes, we had our problems but . . . he just wasn't like that. He'd never just abandon his business and his family and everything he cared about."

"Has your husband ever been diagnosed with depression or any other kind of mental illness?"

"No," I said curtly, annoyed that he was still pursuing this line of questioning. "He didn't just leave us. Something is wrong. Something has happened."

"I'm sorry, Mrs. Wylie," he said. "We need to consider every possibility. The last person who claims to have seen your husband was the owner of the New Haven health-food store in Billings, Montana. Then there's the call to Ed Gallagher in Boise at 5:45 P.M. Beyond that, there've been no reports of an accident involving a pickup fitting this description, and no reports of one being abandoned. No John Does. Nothing after that phone call at 5:45. We're continuing to check the surrounding areas—Wyoming, Colorado, Oregon, and Washington. I'll fax these photographs to the various departments. You'll hear from me the minute there're any developments."

The interview seemed to end rather abruptly. Maybe that's just the way it was supposed to work. What more was he supposed to ask? And yet I felt sure I could read his mind. He'd already drawn his own conclusions. Same old story. Man abandons his family in search of a better life. More than likely he'd seen it a hundred times. If I had been in his position, I might have drawn the same . . . But it wasn't true! It couldn't be true.

As he left my house and drove away, I had the dark feeling that I might never hear from the police again.

* * *

My body was still. My heart beat slowly, pulsing like a metronome. I hadn't moved all day. Hadn't even twitched a muscle. Not since I'd first awakened and tried to slake my thirst with another scoop of snow from the drift pressing against the driver's-side window. My hunger pangs may have dissipated, but my thirst was excruciating. I couldn't quench it. I'd repeatedly resorted to eating pure snow. But I could never eat it fast enough and my tongue and throat went so numb that I tasted blood.

The day was dim and overcast. A thick fog had crept over the truck. I suspected it had risen from the surface of a lake or stream at the bottom of the gorge, but I couldn't be sure. It had been quite warm today. That afternoon the snow in my cup had started to melt on its own. There'd been no need to fire up the engine. Which was good. Because only a little over a quarter tank of gas remained.

I fought to keep my head clear. The thing I feared most was my own imagination. There had been voices in the dark. Disjointed. Sometimes laughing. Sometimes rebuking. Like in dreams during a high fever, I could never put the words together.

Now all was quiet. I could no longer hear the wolves, but I knew they were there. They'd been stalking around the truck for the last two days. At least I think it had been two days. Time had no meaning anymore. These past nine days might as well have been ninety.

Now and then I thought I could see dark shapes in the fog, crouching in the snow, moving restlessly among the drifts, waiting in earnest for my next mistake. The black one was still there as well. Once in the night I'd opened my eyes and perceived something glowing through the windshield, like burning candles. One flick of the wipers revealed the hulking wolf, yellow eyes still full of hate. When it knew I had seen it, it leaped away. Or maybe it just faded into the darkness.

I tried not to think about the wolves. I was safe at the moment. They couldn't get inside the truck. This was my sanctuary. My hallowed ground. No demons could penetrate here.

I thought about the drifter, my first hallucination. The start of it all. I thought about his bewildering question. The words continued to echo:

"If this were your last Christmas, who would you spend it with? The choice is yours. You can spend it with anyone."

Anyone.

Anyone at all.

I'd given him my answer. Hadn't I? I'd told him I wanted to spend it with my family? Was there any other choice? What else could I have ever hoped? It just wasn't meant to be. The drifter's question had been meant to taunt me, like everything else. One long laugh in the belly of God.

I realized I hadn't really given the drifter a firm answer. I'd left it open. I said I'd have to think about it. He'd said something else. Something strange. What was it?

"Some things we don't have any choice about. Other things . . . our choices might even save our life."

What a strange thing to say. What was it supposed to mean? My choice for Christmas might save my life? It made no sense. Just rambling. Like all the other voices in the dark. Nonsense. And yet . . .

Something about the question gnawed at me. I couldn't get it out of my head. There was something mystical about it. Something premonitory. Here I was, at the edge of death. If anyone needed rescuing, it was me. I'd lost all faith in search parties. All faith that anyone out there really cared to find me. Perhaps the drifter was right. The choice could save my life.

Suddenly I had the answer, and it made me smile. From the brightest corners of my memory loomed the iron-jawed figure of man. "Now there's a choice," I mumbled. "Give me a hero for Christmas. Give me the biggest hero I ever had."

I closed my eyes and reveled in the fantasy. Basked in its glow. After a moment my smile turned down. I realized I felt more lost and alone than I'd ever felt before. I sat back in my seat, prepared to drift off forever. Sleep. It was the only pleasure left. The only escape from the pain.

A moment later my eyes popped open. I peered through the fog at the ghostly outline of the ridge above my pickup. I furrowed my brow. Something was different. I couldn't put my finger on it. As if . . . the air itself was different. Not hotter or colder. Not thicker or thinner. Just . . . different.

My heart starting pounding. The fear of God began to well up in my breast. Something was happening. I could feel it. Heaven help me, I could feel the hallucination coming on before I could see it. I braced myself. And yet nothing happened. All was quiet. I began to feel ridiculous. Nothing had changed. It was all in my mind. All in my imagination.

Then the wolves began to stir.

It started in low—the growling and snarling—and began to build to a frenzied pitch. I pressed my face to the passenger-side window. The wolves were going *nuts!* I could see at least a dozen wolf-like shadows in the fog. They were on their feet, scrambling back and forth, barking and howling like banshees. All of them had their attention riveted on the same place. They peered off into the deeper fog to the west. I watched several leap into the gloom to attack something.

Then I heard the first yelp—bloodcurdling. The cry of death. Whatever they had attacked, it had attacked *back*. I heard another death knell. More wolves sprang into action, savagely determined to kill the unseen enemy. I stiffened with dread. Whatever it was, it had to be more terrible than anything I had yet encountered. The fog rolled. From the mist emerged the outline of a man. An iron-jawed man in a Stetson hat, brandishing a pistol in one hand and a curved hunting knife in the other. I cocked an eyebrow and curled my lip. What the heck was going on?

The man was knee-deep in snow, fighting off each canine attacker in turn. I jolted as I heard the pistol discharge. One of the shadowy gray wolves went limp in mid-flight and tumbled at the man's feet. Another landed on the man's back, knocking off his hat, but he swung around and tossed the animal back into the drift. The pistol fired again, and then again. The yelping wolves continued to pile up around him.

As the last of the lunging wolves collapsed lifelessly onto the drift and the survivors retreated into the fog, the iron-jawed cowboy stood up tall. He gave the pistol a twirl and slid it back into its holster. He re-sheathed the knife and retrieved his hat, slapping it once or twice to remove the snow. Then he pulled it snugly over his brow, sliding two fingers along the brim. Finally he started toward the truck.

Panic set in. I wrenched backwards, pressing hard against the driver's-side door. The cowboy's face peered back at me through the passenger-side window. *A demon!* A wraith in disguise! It couldn't get in. Not if I didn't let it. This was my sanctuary. My—

His hand pulled up on the door handle.

I tried to yell. Nothing came out. My lungs were frozen. The man kicked his snowy boots a time or two on the rim and slid into place on the passenger seat, slamming the door behind him.

"*Whew!*" he declared, shaking his head. "Nasty critters! Real ornery tempers. That oughta fix 'em though. Don't expect they'll be back anytime soon."

I said nothing, my eyes like silver dollars. I remained

stiff and still, my heart throbbing in both ears. He took off one of his rawhide gloves and offered me his hand.

"Name's Weymouth. Sterling Weymouth."

I didn't budge. My eyes squinted, scanning his features like lasers. Recognition set in with a gasp. It *couldn't* be! What was happening? I couldn't believe it! It was Sterling "Dead-eye" Weymouth! The demons had transformed, transmogrified, metamorphosed—they'd taken on the form of my childhood hero!

His hand hung there. He realized I wasn't going to take it.

"What's the matter, son? You look a bit pale."

I was beside myself. "What are you *doing* here?!"

He pulled off the other glove. With a heavy sigh he sat back and said, "Don't rightly know. I was hopin' you might give me the skinny on that. There I was, doin' what I always do, and next thing I know—*bamm!*—I'm up to my armpits in wolves. If this is a nightmare, it's the most bizarre nightmare I ever had. You ever hear of a nightmare so cold it'd freeze your keister to a tree?"

I shook my head.

"Only thing I can figure is I've died and gone to hell, just like my third wife said I would."

I blinked my eyes, still unbelieving. Sterling Weymouth! It had to be a mirage. There was no one on the seat beside me. It was all in my head! I hadn't seen a movie with Sterling Weymouth in thirty years! Once he'd torn up the screen with the likes of Gary Cooper and John Wayne. Then he became the king of B-movie adventures—*"Gunfighter's Gold," "Attack of the Killer Samurai,"* and *"Tarzan Meets Billy the Kid."* I couldn't have counted the hours I'd spent in the peeling vinyl chairs of the Cody Theater mesmerized by his every word and move. He looked the same, just the way he'd been immortalized in my memory. Shouldn't he have been in his seventies or eighties? My head felt ready to burst. The ageless idol of my youth was sitting right beside me, blowing warm air into his palms and demanding, "You got any heat in this bucket of bolts or do I have to light the seat on fire?"

His eyes indicated the ignition. Fumbling, I turned the key and started the engine. Then I faced him again with the same mixture of mortification and awe.

"How long before this tub starts blowin' hot instead of cold?" he asked.

"A m-minute or two." I swallowed. "You can't be real. None of this is real—"

Weymouth grabbed my collar and gave me a firm slap on the cheek, just sharp enough to wake me out of my stupor and just stiff enough to convince me that this was no dream.

"Snap out of it, pardner!" he barked. "I need you to tell me what's goin' on. I got things to do. Places to be. Where in blazes are we and how do I get outa here?"

"We're—"

"What's that? Speak up!"

"We're in Wyoming. Beartooth Pass. I'm . . . stranded."

"Stranded? How? You blow a tire?"

"No. Slid off the road."

"I see. Lousy break. I feel for you, son. Really. But that don't tell me squat about how I got here."

"I think I . . . *wished* you here."

"You what?"

I sank heavily into the seat and screwed my palms into the sockets of my eyes. "This doesn't make any sense. None of this makes any sense!"

"*Wished* me here?" he repeated. "You gotta be kiddin' me. Why'd you go and do that?"

"I . . . I don't know. I didn't mean . . . I was just rambling and—"

"How long am I supposed to stay?"

"I think . . . through Christmas."

Weymouth was dumbstruck. "*Christmas!* That's six days away! You mean to tell me I'm supposed to sit here with you in this truck for six whole days? How am I—? Who in tarnation—? I'll go *stir crazy!* I gotta have a smoke." He began feeling through the pockets of his buckskin jacket. He came up empty. "You got any smokes?"

I shook my head.

He cursed up a storm. "*No smokes!* What *do* you have? Deck of cards? Bottle of spirits? What in perdition are we supposed to do for six days?!"

I opened and closed my mouth, unsure how to reply.

"How long have *you* been up here?"

"Nine days, I think."

"*Nine days!* What have you been eatin'?"

I shook my head again, slowly.

Now he was *really* flabbergasted. "You mean to tell me you ain't eaten in nine days? You mean to tell me yer starvin' to death?"

I nodded.

"And—oh, this is choice!—you 'wished' me here so I could *starve to death with you?!*"

I frowned heavily. "No, I didn't want that at all—"

"What did you expect? Did you think I'd bring my own take-out? I'll tell you somethin' right now, son. There's no way I'm gonna stay here for six days and starve to death with you. How could you just sit here like this? Why in Sam Hill haven't you tried to hike out?"

"What do you mean? There's five feet of snow out—"

"*Yer starvin' to death, boy!* What kind of a man are you? You wanna die in here like some shriveled-up pantywaist or die like a man, out there in the elements? Don't you got any guts? Don't you think it's at least worth a try?"

I was flustered. My childhood hero was calling me a shriveled-up pantywaist. "I thought it was just a matter of time. They always say, never leave your vehicle—"

"That's *wimp* talk, boy! Any man worth his salt woulda been outa here the very first day. Now what about you? Do you really wanna spend Christmas sittin' here like a lump of mold, or do you wanna spend it eatin' a three-inch T-bone at my cattle ranch in Sun Valley, Idaho?"

"But . . . you don't understand. I have no strength. Maybe the first day I might have *tried*, but not now. Nine days. No food. I can hardly stand, let alone—"

"I didn't ask for excuses. I asked what you *wanted*."

I stared into his hard-set eyes. The words came back to me: *Other choices could save your life.* Was this really my opportunity? My singular chance? After all, this was *Sterling Weymouth!* The toughest man I'd ever heard tell of—even off the big screen. Fan magazines claimed he was a real-life bronco buster, Golden Gloves boxer, and a dead-aim with any firearm. But even the toughest man ever born could never plow his way for thirty miles through five feet of snow.

"It's impossible," I persisted. "We'd never make it."

He leaned forward, eyes blazing like fire. "All you gotta do is say the word. Just tell me what you want."

In the face of that, how else could I have answered? "I want a steak," I replied. "I want a T-bone steak."

A wide, trademark grin climbed his cheeks. "Well, all right then. Leave it to me."

He reached for the door.

"What are you doing?" I asked, panicked.

"Just hang tight. I'll be back."

The cowboy shut the door and disappeared into the fog. I sat there in the blizzard of my own thoughts. I continued to sit for a long time. As the fog thickened into night, I began to wonder if any encounter had taken place at all. Was it just a figment of my tortured imagination? After all, everything was back to normal again. The night was just as cold. My muscles continued to ache with lethargy and bruises. My thirst was more insatiable than ever.

As I stared out the window, I could still make out the shadows of the dead wolves. That left me with two options—either the encounter had been real, or my hallucination had never really ended. I wasn't sure which I would have preferred.

The howl of a wolf floated down from the hills like a distant foghorn. I hadn't seen the carcass of the black monster among all the others strewn about my pickup. The lupus was still out there. And, I felt certain, it was still hunting.

SUNDAY, DECEMBER 20

Day 10

"What did they say, Mom?" asked Zackary. "What did the police find out?"

"Nothing yet," I said, trying to sound brave. "They said they still haven't heard from some of the state offices. They said it's still too soon."

"They're really not doing anything, *are they?"*

I couldn't blame him for his frustration. I felt it as well. But how could I blame the police? What more could they do? Their dockets were probably filled with missing persons, most of whom had left of their own accord. How could I expect them to focus all their efforts on one person? To them he was just a photograph, a name on a page. To me he was my husband, the father of my children.

"I'm sure they're doing all they can," I told my kids.

"Sure they are," said Zack sarcastically. "Those guys couldn't find a crack in the sidewalk."

He stomped out of the room. His little brother followed, leaving only Tamara, who looked very apprehensive.

"Mom," she asked, "do you think . . . I mean . . . You

don't think he might have . . . gone away, do you?"

She'd overhead my conversation yesterday with the investigator. This question had probably haunted her all through the night.

"No," I said firmly. Nevertheless, my voice sounded tired. Even to me it betrayed a shred of doubt.

Tears came to Tamara's eyes.

I drew her into an embrace. "Oh, my angel. It's all right. Your father would never leave us."

"Are you sure?"

"Of course I'm sure. He loves us with all his heart."

She was sobbing freely now. "But you guys fight every day. You fight all the time."

"I'm sorry, honey. We'll do better from now on. I promise we'll do better. Just as soon as he comes home."

"But what if he never does?"

"He will," I insisted. "Don't ever believe anything different."

"How do you know, Mom? You can't know something like that. How do you know?"

"I know because we'll never stop looking. No matter what. We'll do anything it takes. Anything."

"Like what?" Tamara asked. "What else can we do?"

I sighed. That's where I was stumped. There were no more phone calls to make. No more leads to pursue. And yet there had to be something else. Something we hadn't thought of. I had to discover what it was. An idea struck me.

"We can pray," I told my daughter. "We can ask Heavenly Father to tell us what we should do."

My daughter looked at me strangely, and yet it was only a moment later that her eyes glittered with a new-found hope. That night, we all knelt together. Each of us took our turn reciting a prayer out loud. Even Zackary, who at first had seemed the most reluctant, opened his mouth and opened his heart to God. The prayers weren't very long, that is, all but Corban's, who might have gone on forever if Tamara hadn't cleared her throat to indicate that it was her turn. The event seemed to give the children comfort. As for me, I wasn't sure what I felt. I guess I felt comforted too, not so much by a belief that our prayers would produce the desired result, but comforted with the feeling—no, the conviction—*that as we knelt there, we were truly joined by the presence of something wonderful, enwrapping us in its arms, and listening.*

* * *

"On your feet! We're burnin' daylight!"

My eyelids fluttered open. The mug of Sterling Weymouth fell into focus only after great effort, like turning the focal ring on a camera too far. He was standing outside in his tall gray Stetson, looking in through the open passenger-side door. He appeared as much "larger-than-life" now as he ever had on the silver screen.

I tried to not act as shocked as I had the day before, yet I confess, I was still feeling overwhelmed. The surreal quality to the air persisted. I was sure a few shakes of the head might make him disappear. So I tried it. It didn't work. "Dead-Eye" Weymouth reached into the cab.

"Come on! Let's go!" He sounded like a cattle driver. "Time to earn your grub, cowboy. We got a long ways to go before sundown."

He dragged me across the bench like an old coat and stood me up in the snow. My knees started to buckle. He caught me and leaned me back against the hood until I could gather my strength.

As I waited for the world to stop spinning, he declared, "Pull yourself together, son! This is the day we make a man out of you. No fan of mine wimps out with his back against the wall. He keeps fightin'. Even if it costs him his life. Nothin' more noble than dyin' with your head held high, knowin' you gave it all you got. Now tie these on."

To my surprise, there were two sets of snowshoes at our feet. They'd been constructed from pine boughs and tied together with rawhide. Was this what Weymouth had been doing all night? I looked at him in wonder. The pine trees were only thirty yards down the gorge. I'd had plenty of twine in my camper. I might have built these things myself if . . . if it had occurred to me.

"You see?" said Weymouth. "You had a way outta here all the time. You just weren't usin' yer nugget!" He jabbed two fingers into my forehead.

Hope began welling in my breast. Maybe we *could* walk out of here. Maybe I *would* be having a Christmas steak with Sterling Weymouth at his ranch in Idaho. Was it possible? Could my hallucination actually save my life? It was all so utterly bizarre, so totally impossible. And yet here I was, strapping on snowshoes designed by Sterling Weymouth. Here I was, prepared to venture off into the wilderness with my body engulfed in lethargy. Maybe Weymouth wasn't a demon, but an angel, a heavenly messenger in disguise. He was probably the only person in the universe who could have convinced me to do something so completely outlandish.

It was a warm day, overcast. The sun was a pale, white ball in the eastern sky as we set out across the barren snowfield. Weymouth led the way. He'd given me a walking stick made from an old mangled branch. It worked just like a crutch in case I was about to collapse, which in the beginning occurred about every fifteen steps. But hope is a funny thing. An incredible thing. I kept telling myself all I had to do was take one more step. And then one more. I could do this! I could really do it!

And yet for Weymouth, I wasn't doing it nearly fast enough.

"Come on, boy!" he called back from twenty yards ahead. "You've been slackin' now for ten days! Get the lead out!"

He was like an obnoxious drill sergeant. And yet if he really was saving my life, it was worth all the abuse he could dish out. He was leading me down into the gorge. At one point, after fighting off a dizzy spell, I turned back to look at my truck. Seeing it from a distance of about a hundred yards, it was easy to understand how a plane might miss it. It looked just like any other snow-covered boulder resting against the ridge.

Weymouth was about fifty yards ahead now, making his way down into the gorge by way of a narrow sloping shelf. I scrunched my forehead in confusion. Just a short distance further, the icy cliffs would become almost sheer. Just where did he think he was going?

He waved me onward. "Let's go! We don't have all day!"

Swallowing, I trudged forward. But after another fifteen steps, I had to stop again. I sat back in the snow.

"What's the matter?" Weymouth gruffed.

"Have to rest," I panted.

"Rest?! Ain't you had enough rest? Let's move! Let's move!"

His voice sounded distorted. I felt faint. Water. I needed water. I had no gloves. I reached out from inside the cuff of my sweater and grabbed a mouthful of snow. I let it melt on my tongue and around my face. Weymouth had stopped to wait for me.

I hoisted myself back up with the walking stick. When I reached Weymouth, forty yards later, it was all I could do to keep from falling flat on my face. I sat down in the snow again, my breaths coming in deep pants.

"Son, at this rate we're not gonna make it a single mile," he complained. "You gotta reach deep down. Reach down to your ankles if you have to. But do it! And do it *now!*"

I felt myself growing angry. "Why did you come this way? This is the hardest way we could have gone! Why didn't we stick to the highway?"

"Stick to the highway? What's the matter with you? You grow up in a Sunday suit? Never got dirt under your fingernails? Any lily-livered milksop could stick to the highway. You and I are goin' *overland*. As the crow flies! The way *real* men would do it."

"You gotta be kidding. You mean to tell me we're going this way because you think this is the way *real men* would go?"

He stuck a scolding finger in my face. "I sense a note of sarcasm in your voice, boy, and I don't like it. You gotta trust me. You gotta *believe* in me. Now, who's in charge? Me or you? It can't be both of us. Which is it gonna be?"

My chest fell. How could I be questioning my hero? I was in no condition to be in charge of anything. I closed my eyes and drew a few more breaths. "You. You're in charge."

"That's better. Now on your feet. Up! Up!"

With every muscle quaking, I pulled myself to my feet and continued on. After a while I was practically walking blind. I kept my focus on the tracks made by Weymouth's snowshoes. I knew the terrain was insanely steep and dangerous, but I refused to let my focus stray. I could hear a river. I hadn't been aware that there *was* a river this high in the Beartooths. But the sound was unmistakable. When at last I raised my eyes, Weymouth was nowhere in sight. His tracks had disappeared around an outcropping of the ridge. I realized in an instant that I should have kept my focus on the ground. The mere act of raising my eyes caused an unstoppable wave of delirium.

My eyes rolled back in my head. I was losing my balance. For a moment it felt good, as if I were flying. When I hit the snow it was like settling into a bed of cottony pillows. But then my body began to tumble. I was falling! Toppling end over end! My body twisted into a full airborne spin, crashing into the surface and sending up explosions of powder. One of my snowshoes flew past my vision, broken and tattered. Above me I could hear rumbling, as if an earthquake were following me to the bottom of the gorge.

My final landing came with a crunch. Pain shot up my spine. Still, it was softer than I might have expected, broken by a cushion of deep snow. Mounds of additional snow began piling on top of me! My arms grasped desperately upwards. Within seconds the avalanche covered me up to my neck. Then a final heavy clump landed on top of my head.

I experienced a terrible, strangling moment. I couldn't move except for the fingers of one of my outstretched hands. Suddenly I became aware of someone laughing. Laughing as heartily and merrily as I'd ever heard anyone laugh.

My fingers were gripped by a human hand. The snow was scooped away from my face. Another hand latched onto the back of my collar. With a mighty heave I was yanked from the mound of snow and left to lay helplessly at the foot of my rescuer. As I looked up through the flakes on my eyelashes, there stood Sterling Weymouth, still splitting a gut.

"That's *one* way to come down the mountain, pardner! Not the way I'd a' chosen, but just as effective!"

I'd almost broken my neck and this guy thought it was the knee-slappin'est thing he'd ever seen!

"Can I help ya up?"

I shook my head.

"Ah, c'mon. You ain't hurt. You didn't fall far enough to break a toenail. Now, let's go. Gimme yer hand."

What was he *talking* about! I'd just tumbled over a hundred feet! Both snowshoes had been ripped off my feet. My body was crusted in snow. My stomach ached with a fresh wave of nausea. I clenched my fist into a ball to keep him from taking it. I was *not* getting up.

"What's your problem?" he gruffed. "I watched every inch of that fall. I know when a man's been hurt. And you, son, don't qualify. You just gonna lay there all day? The best part of the journey's still waitin' for us. Come on! From here on out it's an easy boat ride to civilization."

For the first time I realized that the roar of the river was loud and clear. I bent my neck to the side. I couldn't believe it. I'd tumbled right to the banks of a pristine mountain watercourse. The river cut a sleek and bubbling pathway through an opalescent valley lined with fir trees and aspens.

I furrowed my brow in befuddlement. This was impossible. The only river around here was the Clarks Fork of the Yellowstone, and that was still twenty miles south. Something else struck me. Did he say *boat ride*? A quick glance up and down the banks revealed no boat.

"What are you talking about?" I demanded.

"I'm talkin' about floatin' our way to freedom, boy! I'm talkin' about a one-way trip to T-bone paradise! You and me and the setting sun!"

What was he going to do? Take that big ol' hunting knife and chop down a couple dozen trees to make a raft? His rawhide glove was still reaching out for me. I looked in his eyes. Was anything impossible for him? After all, he'd made snowshoes from pine branches. Maybe he could drum up a boat just as miraculously. Like a lost soul in the trance of a television evangelist, I reached out for that hand and let him pull me to my feet. He'd been right about my fall. There were no serious injuries. Just a large new bruise on my rear and a slightly twisted right ankle.

He set me down on an ice shelf jutting several yards out over the river. The icy, clear water captivated my attention. I leaned over the edge to drink. Several inches broke off and floated away. I backed up a bit and laid flat, then I set my lips in the mountain-sweet nectar. I was still drinking when I felt the first shock wave in the earth.

I hesitated a full second before craning my neck to see what had caused it. Then my eyes widened in horror. Weymouth was jumping! He was bringing the full weight of his snowshoes down on the shelf of ice. He was trying to *break it loose!*

"Are you crazy?!" I screamed.

He wasn't paying attention. Instead, he drew his pistol and blasted six bullet holes along the length. I shielded my face from the flying ice chips. After emptying his gun, he made one final mighty leap— bringing his snowshoes a good foot and a half off the ice—and came down with a mighty "Heeaww!"

Icy water washed up over my already-frozen hands as the shelf splashed into the river and broke away from shore. Weymouth used my walking stick to push us out into the swiftest part of the current. My mind was ready to curl in on itself, give in, fade to black. I looked into Weymouth's face as if he were a complete lunatic. He stared down the tree-lined valley with a look of pure satisfaction, teeth gritted for the adventure of a lifetime.

"Hang onto your skirts, boys and girls! We'll be ridin' this dogie to hell and back again!"

"You're nuts, Weymouth! Do you hear me! Totally certifiable!"

He gave me a cockeyed grin. "What was you expectin', son? You made a wish to spend Christmas with "Dead-eye" Weymouth! I'll see you get yer money's worth for that ticket or die trying. You ain't seen nothin' yet!"

A shudder rippled through my body. I'd left the security of my pickup to venture off with a madman! There was no way this slab of ice could stay afloat. Water was washing over the top even now, making the surface as slick as snot. There was white water ahead! Even if I could swim to shore, I'd be dead from exposure in a matter of minutes!

Out of the corner of my eye I saw something that seemed to clinch my fate. For a split second the raven-black wolf appeared on the right bank, running stealthily from one tree to the next. It was following us—following *me*, still determined to have my soul.

Weymouth used the stick to guide us through the first snarl of rapids. "Here we go!" he shouted.

I dug my bloodless fingertips into the surface of the ice shelf as we tumbled into a deep water chasm and shot out the other side. The front of my coat and pants were drenched in the melee. Sterling Weymouth whooped and slapped his hip, as if riding a bucking bronco. As the ice slab spun around, ready to be pulled into its next dip, I vomited the majority of the water I'd drunk. For several seconds, I lost consciousness. I reawakened just before sliding off completely, and kicked my legs to find the center again.

To my relief, the river went smooth after that. We were now floating serenely in the current.

"That wasn't so bad," said Weymouth, unruffled. "Hardly even raised my pulse. Let's hope the next one rides like a Coney Island roller coaster."

"I want off," I muttered, my face pressed to the ice.

"What's that?"

"Off," I repeated. "I want off."

"'Fraid I can't accommodate you, son—even if I wanted to. We don't exactly have a paddle. River's too deep here for this ol' stick."

"Then find a place!" I shouted. "Fast!"

"You know what your problem is, boy? You plum forgot how to have fun! I'm makin' an adventurer outta you, and you ain't showin' the least bit of gratitude."

"I want out of here!" I proclaimed. "I want out *now!*"

"Well, if that don't beat all. That's loyalty for ya. If I thought you was even half a man, I'd take you by the scruff of the neck and kick the livin'—"

Weymouth stopped in mid-sentence. He was gaping straight ahead, the picture of surprise. I knew the cause of his astonishment even before I saw it. I could hear it roaring like a stampede of cattle. I pushed myself up on both knees to appreciate the full horror of the spectacle. It was a waterfall. *Of course* it was a waterfall! I was with Sterling Weymouth! There *had* to be a waterfall!

I faced Weymouth. "What do we do now?"

He shrugged, almost casually. "Looks like we're gonna have to take it."

"*What?!*"

"We're gonna ride it out, son. Hold on to yer hat!"

"But we'll be killed!"

"I expect you're right. But it'll be one rip snortin' way to go out. Won't it?"

My mind imploded with terror. I was going to die! I glanced back at the waterfall, dragging us relentlessly into its jaws. *We'd be over it in twenty seconds or less!*

I faced Weymouth again. "But I believed in you! You said to trust you!"

He cocked his head, looking quizzical. "Trust *me?* Why in the name of Sam Hill would you wanna go trustin' me? I told you from the beginning how this might turn out. You believe everything you see in the movies?"

I fell back on my haunches, as if slapped in the face. The falls loomed closer. *Ten more seconds!*

"What have I done!" I mourned. "What have I done!"

There was a sudden twinkle in Weymouth's eye. "Change your mind?"

"Huh?"

"About Christmas. Sounds like yer regrettin' yer choice."

"Yes!" I cried. "*I change my mind!*"

Weymouth grinned. "Then I got one piece of advice, son."

"What?"

"JUMP!"

With that, Weymouth grabbed me by the belt and flung me over the side with all his might. I braced myself for the cold shock of my life. But instead the wind was knocked from my lungs. I hadn't landed in the water. My chin had been bruised by a knot of wood. I'd come down on a log jam at the edge of the waterfall. Only my legs were immersed.

I raised my eyes in time to see the slab of ice fly over the falls with Sterling Weymouth shouting "Yeeeeehawww!" at the top of his lungs. The ice chunk fell into the mist and disappeared from my view. I pulled myself up far enough to see all fifty feet down to the bottom. The ice crashed against the rocks, flying apart like a plate of china. But Weymouth was nowhere in sight. I gawked in total mystification. He couldn't have fallen ahead of the ice. The cowboy had vanished before impact.

Suddenly I understood. Once I'd repealed my choice, the cowboy had been released. I was alone again. Alone with no prospects for the future except to freeze to death on the banks of a raging river.

Day 11

"We need to go there," Zackary proclaimed.

"Go where?" I asked.

"To Montana. We need to look for him ourselves."

"Zack's right," said Tamara. "The police aren't doing anything, We need to follow his footsteps—go every place he went."

"Yes!" Corban concurred. "We need to go to Montana! Please, Mom. Please!"

"Oh, kids," I said, sitting down, feeling overwrought. "Do you realize what you're saying? Do you realize how much area we're talking about? Hundreds of miles. It would be like looking for a needle in a haystack. A needle in a hundred haystacks."

"I don't care," said Zack. "It's better than sitting here doing nothing."

"We have to do something," said Tamara. "You promised we'd do everything we could. We'll let the police know where we are if they happen to find out something first."

It was obvious my children had put a lot of thought into this. Corban's fingers were intertwined in the act of begging, and he was bouncing up and down on his toes. I let the idea sink in. Somehow it filled me with courage. There was one argument I couldn't deny. It was *better than sitting here doing nothing.*

"All right," I said.

The children sent up a cheer. The enthusiasm was contagious. I felt a flutter in my heart. A surge of determination. What did we have to lose?

"Pack up!" cried Zackary. "We're going to Montana!"

"Wait," I said, trying to temper the mood with a dose of reality. "Please, listen for a minute. We'll go. We'll look. We'll do everything we can. But I don't want you to get your hopes up. I don't want you to be disappointed."

"But hope is all we have," said Tamara.

I smiled painfully. "We might not be back for Christmas."

"That's okay," said Corban. "I already know what I want. I want my dad."

* * *

The shivering had finally stopped. For the last several hours it had been uncontrollable, nearly rattling my teeth from their foundations. The chill had reached into every muscle, seemingly congealing the blood itself into particles of ice. But the shivering was gone now. I was still alive. Alive, and finally warm.

I'd seen the cave from the banks of the river. It was about twenty feet away, nestled in a crag of rocks. The entrance was only three feet wide and nearly overgrown with branches and brambles. I'd crawled on my hands and knees through the ice and snow to reach it. At first I'd thought I might meet up with a hibernating grizzly—it would have been just my luck. But the den was empty—although it was strewn with leaves and twigs from some animal resident of the past.

I'd discovered in my shirt pocket the same book of matches that I'd stuffed there on the first day of my ordeal. Somehow it had remained high and dry while the front of my winter coat had been drenched. I'd managed to gather some dry branches that had been sitting just inside the cave's mouth. But when I went to strike a match, it wouldn't ignite. My fingers were shaking too badly. I broke off one match head after another. I was down to my last three when I finally got one to light. I cared for that flame like a nursing mother, carefully nourishing and feeding it with larger and larger twigs.

At last I'd built up a sizable conflagration right at the cave's entrance and pulled in every ounce of spare wood in the immediate vicinity to keep it going for the next several hours. After that I'd stripped off all my shreds of wet clothing and set them around the fire's perimeter. As the sky had darkened into night, I curled up in my underwear against the cold stone at the back of the cave, shivering like a madman and watching steam rise off my wet clothing. I'd fallen asleep wondering if I'd ever reawaken, wondering if I was settling into the sleep of death brought on by freezing.

Don't ask me how I survived the night. My body had tapped into an ancient store of strength, something

I'd inherited from some virtually forgotten ancestor, perhaps my mother's great-grandfather who'd pulled a handcart across the Wyoming plains. As I stirred occasionally to feed the fire, I marveled that I was still breathing, still moving, and that my fingers and toes weren't yet black with frostbite.

Sometime after midnight I was awakened by a low growl. It came from beyond the entrance of the cave. I peered past the licking flames and saw the narrow yellow eyes of the wolf. I pressed deeper into the back wall, cringing like cornered prey. But for now, the fire kept the demon at bay. Finally it moved on, though I knew it would likely be back as soon as my flame went cold.

My head felt hot with fever. I tossed and turned until the last hour of night, replaying the extraordinary events of the past two days in my thoughts. My choice had been a mistake. I realized that now. I'd selected a fantasy. An illusion. What I needed was a *real* hero for my last Christmas. But real heroes in the course of my life had been hard to come by.

I'd burned so many bridges. Taken for granted so many of those who'd tried to love me. Christmas was a sacred day—I couldn't force anyone to spend it with me if they didn't want to. Even my family. I firmly believed I'd lost them. I had no right to cause them any more pain.

God, what had I done? What had I sacrificed?

I felt a tremendous pang of self-loathing, followed by a crushing loneliness. I felt so empty. My last Christmas. What did it matter? There was no one, literally no one. I would spend it alone. That would be best. Then I couldn't hurt anyone else. I closed my eyes and started to sob like a little child. A child who's lost everything in this world. A child who's lost . . .

My heart skipped a beat. In that instant I knew who I wanted to be with for my last Christmas. Surviving—saving my own life—no longer mattered. And yet even as I uttered the name, even as I cried it into the wind, I felt I'd gone beyond the mark. I'd asked for too much.

My eyes popped open. The sunlight was shining though the entrance, defined by sharp and penetrating beams. The quality of the air had changed again. I cocked an ear. *How strange*, I thought. Where was the roar of the waterfall? That mellowing rumble had been my constant companion throughout the night. But now the sound was gone. The air had become as silent and still as an empty cathedral.

I reached out for my pants and coat. The act of moving was like bending a dry branch, as if all my joints might splinter and split. My clothing was still slightly damp, but I bore the chill. After dressing as quickly as I could, I crawled carefully over the top of the cooling coals and shimmied my way out.

The river was gone! The whole *scene* had transformed. But it was not unfamiliar. I recognized the ridge behind me and the sloping granite gorge to the north. Off to the right, about forty yards, sat my old Ford pickup and camper, still three-fourths buried in the drifts. I stood there entranced for several moments. It didn't make sense, not unless my entire adventure with Sterling Weymouth had only taken me forty yards from my point of origin. It was like awakening from a dream. There were no snowshoe prints. No carcasses of dead wolves. The hallucinations were over. I was seeing only reality.

No, it wasn't true. Someone was sitting inside the cab of my truck. Through the icy circle on the passenger-side window I could see the figure moving.

My heart started thumping like a drum. I began fighting my way through the deep drifts of snow. *It was him! I knew it was him!* I plunged forward. Somehow I was sure if I didn't move quickly, the image would disappear into the snowdrifts. I would lose it forever.

But it was no use. As I got to within fifteen feet of the truck, I fell. My breath was spent. Energy vanquished. Only fifteen feet left. Still, I'd faltered. *Get up!* I told myself. *You can't give up now!* It was hopeless. My limbs were worthless. I'd gone as far as I could go.

But then the passenger door opened. The figure emerged. My eyes traveled up his body. He was dressed in a heavy brown parka with a thick fur lining around the hood. On the seat behind him lay an army-green backpack with a frayed strap. The drifter. The hitchhiker. I was completely bewildered. This wasn't what I'd asked for. But then, peering into the shadow created by that massive hood, I perceived the vague contour of his face. He was smiling. I knew that smile. I remembered it so well.

The figure came forward until he stood directly over me. I gaped up at him, thunderstruck, the lump in my throat as large as a mountain. He offered me his hand. I took it unquestioningly, unhesitatingly. He brought me to my feet as easily as any seven-year-old boy might be lifted by the hand of his hero. His *first* hero. The only true hero a boy can ever really have.

"Dad," I cried. "Oh, Dad!"

His hood fell back and we embraced. In that instant all of my secret dreams of the last thirty-four years came true—the dreams of a seven-year-old boy staring for hours out his front room window, hoping that somehow his father might still drive around the corner and pull into the driveway. Then he would come inside and fold me in his arms, wiping away my tears and proving once and for all that the news that had crippled my tiny heart had all been a terrible, terrible lie.

"It's good to see you, Ben," he replied. "It's so good to see you."

TUESDAY, DECEMBER 22

Day 12

The sun was blindingly bright, reflecting off the ice-crusted highway all the way across the Wyoming plains. I'd forgotten my sunglasses. Next gas stop, *I told myself,* I'll buy another pair.

The children were pensive and anxious, better behaved than I'd seen them on any road trip. It was almost unnatural. I almost wished someone would fight or crawl over the seat or spill something. Then I'd know my kids were still kids.

As we passed through the small town of Lander, I began to seriously regret this whole expedition. I wished I'd been prepared enough to have us leave last night, when our enthusiasm was high. Now my doubts were overwhelming. What were we supposed to do when we got there? Where were we supposed to begin?

Zackary had been concentrating on those very issues. "First," he said, "we go to that health-food store in downtown Billings. We talk to the manager and get him to tell us everything he knows. Then we go to the police station. Then we check out all the motels. We go everywhere and talk to everybody. Leave no stone unturned."

"Then," continued Tamara, "we post his picture in every window we can." She'd made about two hundred copies of a flyer with her father's picture on it—a picture from a sales brochure that we'd found in the basement.

"And on every tree," added Corban.

"You can't post flyers on trees," scoffed Zackary.

"Uh-huh," said Corban. "I saw it on TV."

"That's stupid. We'd need over a million."

"Mom?" asked Tamara. "Can we make more copies if we have to?"

"Yes," I said. "We can make as many copies as you want."

"Even a million?" asked Corban.

"Even a million."

I smiled. My heart was flowing with courage again. It didn't take much. Just the determination of a child. So this is why Heavenly Father gives us children, I thought. With children, you can't help but believe in miracles.

* * *

My father stayed with me that entire night. He'd carried me into the cab of the pickup where I quickly fell asleep. When I awakened the following morning, he was still there, seated on the passenger side of the truck, still smiling his warm, enduring smile, and still wearing the big brown parka that I now recognized from some faraway wintertime memory. He listened to every word

I spoke that morning as the sun glistened through the ice crystals on the windshield. He listened with granite patience and unconditional love, just the way I'd always remembered that my father had listened to me.

"Everything fell apart after you left," I told him. "The family was never the same. Mom worked her fingers to the bone. The rest of us worked right along with her. In the end it made no difference. The bank took the motel. We lost everything."

My voice was hoarse, almost a whisper. I barely had the energy to sit up straight and look in his eyes. The truck was running. The last quarter tank of fuel was almost gone. The heaters were operating on high. And yet I still couldn't get warm. It seemed a miracle that I even had the strength to remain conscious. It had been twelve days. Who knew how much time I had left. Every spare second I had in my father's presence was borrowed time. Precious time. And I didn't want to waste a single instant.

"My world fell apart when you died, Dad. It fell apart for everyone. I was so angry at you for so many years for leaving us."

He sighed and patted my knee. "You were awfully young, Ben. A hard age to lose your father. If there was anything I could have done—any way I could have stayed—I would have never left you. Not in a million years. Children need their fathers. They always will. Tell me about *yours*, Ben. Tell me about my grandchildren."

I smiled proudly. I saw their faces as clearly as the light of the sun. "I have three, Dad. Oh, I wish you could meet them. I could have never asked for better kids. Zackary is twelve now. A young man. He's growing up so fast. And Tamara. She's ten, going on sixteen. So beautiful. And *smart*. Smarter than I ever was. Then there's Corban. He's eight. He looks a lot like you, the same curly brown hair. No one has a bigger heart. I miss him so much. I miss them all so much." The tears began to roll down my cheeks. "I'll never see them again. I'll never tell them how much I love them. Oh, Dad. I didn't know. I didn't know how hard it was going to be to die."

My dad shook his head. "No. Dying is easy, son. It may be the easiest thing you'll ever do. It's living that's hard. You know a lot about how to *build* dreams. You just don't know how to *live* them. You can't see them when they're staring you right in the face."

"I can't?"

"No, you can't. Your choices make that clear enough."

"Choices?" I asked. "You mean about who I would spend my last Christmas with?"

"You thought you were making choices for living. Instead, they were choices for dying."

"But," I replied, "I *am* dying."

"You haven't given yourself anything to really live for. Not yet."

"But . . . I chose *you*."

Dad curled up a corner of his mouth. "There, you see? Case in point. I'm already dead."

I looked away mournfully. "That *was* my point, Dad. I don't *have* any other choices." Grief washed over me. "Don't you see? The only living choice I might have made is no longer mine to make. I neglected it too long. I let it die on the vine."

"What did you allow to die, son?"

"My family. My covenants. Mostly I destroyed *her,* my Jillian. I crushed her like a dried flower. Over and over, into smaller and smaller pieces. There's nothing I can do now. I thought I could fix it, but . . . the damage is done. It's what I deserve. They're better off without me."

"Like you were better off without *me?*"

I faltered, then I replied, "That was different. I'm not you, Dad."

"You think your kids know the difference?"

"Sure," I said. "They know the difference. I've never been there for them—not the way you were there for me."

"But I thought you were angry for so many years because I *wasn't* there."

"No, Dad. I mean when you *were* there. When you were with us, you were a real father. I've never been a real father to my kids. I didn't know how. I *forgot* how— that is, if I ever knew."

"You're wrong, son. You're a real father right now. And you always will be. If you've made some mistakes, you gotta do what you can to make it right. And you gotta do it now." My father glanced at the tiny box containing the sapphire necklace, still sitting on the dashboard. "It wasn't a bad idea. New beginnings. You had the right idea all along. But somewhere you lost faith. After all, Christmas is a time for new beginnings. A hope for the future. No better time to make things right than at Christmas."

I picked up the box, turning it over in my hands and clutching it to my chest. Then I met my father's eyes.

"Oh, Dad. If I thought it was possible . . . I'd do anything. Anything to make up for all the pain. I'd give every part of my soul. Just to be with them one last Christmas."

He put his hand on my shoulder and leaned forward, the fires of eternity glowing in his features. "Then make the choice."

I studied his face. My heart was pulsing with warmth. "But I can't, Dad. I'm here with you."

My father smiled tenderly. "Don't worry about me, my boy. I'll always be here. Soon enough you and I will catch every fish there is to catch and visit every star. But this is Christmas. Christmas is for the living. That includes you. You're still alive, Ben. Do all you can, fight to the very last breath, and leave the rest up to the Lord. Remember, Ben. The choice gives you the power. So I'll ask you one last time. If this was your last Christmas—"

"My family." My lip started to quiver. "I want to spend it with my family."

The last thing I remembered was my father's smile, beaming through the mist. I blinked to clear my vision of tears. When I looked again, he was gone. I was sitting alone in the cab of my pickup. Snow was falling again. The gauge on the fuel tank read just a notch above empty.

I sat up straight, longing for my father's presence. I already missed him so much. Steadily, the longing was replaced by a rush of excitement, building and surging. Something wonderful was about to happen. I could feel it. The final vision was about to reveal itself. I waited in childlike faith, still clutching the box containing the necklace.

I squirmed, the nervousness reaching down to my toes. What would I say to my children when they appeared? What would I say to my Jillian? I felt like a kid again. Like a teenager preparing for his first date. I couldn't believe it. I was actually giddy! It was ridiculous. I'd been married to this woman for fourteen years and I couldn't remember ever feeling like this. I knew there was a good chance she wouldn't even talk to me. But it didn't matter. Just to be with them. There was so much that I needed to say.

I continued to wait. The wind started to pick up a little. Some tufts of snow blew up off the surface, whipped into a curl, and then blended back with the drifts. I shifted once more, trying not to feel impatient, but finding it hard to feel anything else.

Anytime, I thought. *Anytime at all.*

An hour passed. Nothing happened. Two hours. Still nothing.

Had I done something wrong? What was going on? Where was my family? It was my last Christmas. I'd made my choice. *I wanted my family!*

Some time later, the engine of the pickup sputtered and died. The fuel was gone. I waited in the silence as the warm air inside the cab cooled, and then turned cold. I stuck the box with the necklace inside my coat and wrapped myself in all of my blankets.

Toward evening the snow stopped falling. The temperature dropped even further. My hopes started to wane. They weren't coming. For whatever reason, the final episode of my vision was not coming to pass. Obviously there was a limit to heaven's generosity and I had crossed it. Darkness overtook my pickup. A thick, palpable darkness that I could feel against my skin, as heavy as the world.

WEDNESDAY, DECEMBER 23

Day 13

"Sorry, Ma'am," said the desk officer. "There's no record of an abandoned pickup with that license plate being found in all of Billings or the surrounding areas."

I sighed drearily. I supposed I should have expected as much. If there had been anything to report, I likely would have heard it when I called home for my messages. For the first time, the children looked thoroughly discouraged. They were just kids, after all. I might have been proud that they'd kept up their spirits for so long.

"Please," I said to the officer. "There must be something else we can do. We've driven all the way from Utah. We've spoken to everyone we can think of. Is there anything else you can suggest?"

The officer started to shake his head. His eyes locked with those of my eight-year-old son, gazing up at him as if he was the only person who could save his father's life. He massaged the back of his neck. "Where have you been putting up those flyers so far?"

"*Grocery stores,*" *said Zack,* "*gas stations, bus stops—all over town. We've put up almost three hundred so far.*"

"*What about* out *of town?*" *he asked.*

"*Not yet,*" *I replied.* "*We weren't quite sure where to start.*"

There was a road map of Montana on the counter, protected under a quarter-inch pane of glass. The officer leaned over it and said thoughtfully, "*Tell me, did your husband like to fill up with gas before leaving town, or was he like me—the kind of guy who first likes to get a few miles under his belt?*"

"*Actually,*" *I said,* "*he didn't like to fill up at all unless the needle was laying right on empty.*" *I smiled to myself, recalling the numerous times that we had run out of fuel and found ourselves stranded because Ben had been so anxious to reach our destination.*

"*In that case,*" *said the officer,* "*you might show that flyer at a few gas stations and mini-markets along the highways out of town. Do you know which route he took home?*"

I shook my head. "*It would have depended if he had any appointments. Otherwise, the shortest route possible.*"

The officer studied the map, running his finger along the various highways. "*It seems to me . . . if I was goin' all the way to Utah I'd take the 72 down into Wyoming and then hook up with I-80 at Rock Springs.*"

"*That's how we came up,*" *said Tamara.*

"*Is that the fastest?*" *I asked.*

He continued to concentrate. "*Or . . . you could go west to Butte and catch the I-15. That way'd be all interstate. Though I'd probably take the shortcut at Cardwell. Of course, if it was summer, you could take the 212 right on through the Park. That'd probably be the fastest. But that way's closed 'til May."*

"When does it close?"

"October or thereabouts. I know it stayed open late this year, but I doubt it was open when your husband was traveling."

"Do you know what day it closed?"

"No, but I could call the highway patrol and find out. Do you want to know?"

I thought about it, then I dismissed it. "No. That's all right."

"Your best bet," the officer concluded, "would be to go west to Butte or south to Rock Springs and hang that flyer at every gas station along the way. Show the clerks his picture. Ask if they remember him. I know it's not much to go on, but . . . it's about all I can tell you."

I continued to stare at the map, almost absently, following along the various lines and tangles. I looked again at Highway 212 to Yellowstone. If only it was summer, I thought. Then I'd know for sure which way he'd gone. It all seemed so futile. Even if I'd known his route exactly, we were still such a long way from resolving anything.

"Thank you," I said to the officer. "We appreciate your time."

* * *

There was a light. A glow. Very faint. It was off to the south, more or less in the same direction outlined by the snow-covered highway, crowning at the very edge of the horizon. I noticed it in the wee hours of the morning, just before sunrise. It was so faint, I might have brushed it off as insignificant. It might have been the glow of a bright star or planetary body that hung right there at the horizon line. I had no way of knowing. I stared at it for a long time. Why hadn't I seen it before? This must have been the first night that was clear enough. If I'd noticed it a week earlier, I might have still done something about it. Now I was too weak. I couldn't even get out of the car, to say nothing of hiking for miles toward something that might turn out to be nothing. I laid my head back down on the seat. There wasn't anything I could do.

And yet I couldn't shake it off. Why was that light tormenting me?

Suddenly I knew why. It was because that light represented something important. Something I wanted so badly it raged in every cell of my body. I wanted to see my family. I needed to be with them. I felt as if I couldn't breathe or think or function without them. No desire had ever consumed me so desperately. Not success. Not wealth. Not ambition. Not recognition— *Why had my vision come to an end!?* Why couldn't Jillian and my three children have melted out of the fog?

I thought I might have figured it out. It was the phrase my father had used: a *living* choice. I was beginning to understand. It was a living choice because it made me want to fight. It made me want to live.

Oh, God, I thought, the prayer inside me raging. *Please, don't let me die. Of all times, not now!*

I had to see them one more time, just to tell them how sorry I was—to shower them with all the love my soul could generate. Especially Jillian, my wounded flower whom I had crushed and ignored and taken for granted. I didn't expect her to return that love. Surely it was too late for that. But she had to know. Even if it was just so she could use it as a knife to drive into my heart. It would be okay. She'd earned the right. At least she would know. I'd never wanted to tell her anything so badly in all our fourteen years together. Why was I being denied the opportunity?

Living choice. The meaning was clear now. This one was not meant to be a vision. This one was meant to be *real*. It wasn't supposed to just *happen*. I was supposed to *bring it about!*

But how? How in the name of heaven was I supposed to do it?

My limbs felt like blocks of cement. My muscles were already dead. It was only my mind that was still alive. I remembered another thing my father had said: *The choice gives you the power.* I clenched my fists in fury. The very thought that I might not be there Christmas morning—holding them, singing carols, healing their wounded hearts—filled me with terrible anguish. *It couldn't happen!*

My mind sank into despair. I thought of the presents I had bought for them in Billings. Would they be opened as part of a funeral ceremony rather than as part of a Christmas morning celebration? Perhaps that's how they would remember me. By the last gifts that I had bought for them. For Jillian it would be the dove-shaped necklace. Of course it would mean new beginnings now. It would be the promise of something I was never able to deliver. Zackary would remember me by a two-stage hobby rocket, a pair of hiking boots, and a shiny new pocketknife—symbols of the activities and adventures we'd never undertaken. For Tamara it would be a Stereo Walkman, a new winter coat, and a bedroom phone, symbolizing . . . oh, who knows. Symbolizing nothing. Material things. Emptiness. For Corban it would be a remote-control Godzilla, an M&M candy dispenser, and a new pair of—

My heart stopped.

My mind reeled backwards.

I starting gasping. What had I done? I couldn't believe it! Thirteen days and not until this moment had it even crossed my mind! All this time it had been right there! Right under my nose! I'd completely forgotten!

An M&M candy dispenser!

I'd bought my youngest son a coin-operated plastic dispenser chock full of peanut M&Ms. There was even a second bag for refills! *Food!* I'd had food in my camper the entire time!

Food meant energy. Energy meant hope. *Oh God, oh God, was it possible?*

I pulled myself to a sitting position. Even that action struck chords of dizziness. I braced myself against the dashboard until the dizziness stopped. I threw off the blankets and reached toward the door handle on the passenger side. I was breathing too fast. *Calm down*, I told myself. If I didn't calm down, I was going to faint dead away.

I opened the door. My legs seemed to creak like rusted tin as I pulled them into position. As I slid out of the cab, I misjudged my ability to support my own weight and collapsed into the snow. I reached for the door handle. My muscles shook with strain as I pulled myself up again. I used the side of the truck to support myself and concentrated hard to keep from fainting. Then I groped my way around to the back of the camper.

At last I arrived. I turned the knob on the camper door and pulled. It wouldn't budge. Snow from the camper's roof had melted and frozen into the grooves. I yanked it again. Nothing. It was frozen solid!

I uttered my first vocal prayer in twenty-nine years. "Please, Heavenly Father! Please let it open!"

I pulled with all my might. The door came loose with a pop. Shards of ice broke free as I fell backwards, landing on my rump. I laughed gleefully, my eyes filling with tears, overwhelmed that for the first time God had granted me a miracle by faith. But the door had only come open about four inches, hampered by the snow at the base. I pried and pulled and yanked at that gap until I'd forced a space wide enough for me to slip through.

Seconds later I'd reached the closet. I opened it and found all of my presents just as I had left them, still wrapped in shiny gold and silver paper. Which one was it? I couldn't remember. I threw several of the presents aside and found one that appeared to be just the right shape. Then I tore off the wrapping.

My heart did a spinning cartwheel at the sight of the rainbow of colors inside that plastic bubble. Chocolate and peanuts and sugar and preservatives and Red Dye No. 40 and all of the things a growing boy could ever love! I tore open the cardboard package and held the bubble in my hands. I turned it over and looked at the bottom. My fingers were shaking. In my condition there was no way I could pry off that opening. Not when I couldn't even force my eyes to stay focused anymore. I might have smashed it against the edge of the counter and sent an explosion of M&Ms throughout the camper. But fortunately, I had the refill bag wrapped inside the same package. That's where my fingers went next.

Awkwardly, I ripped it open. A few of the candies bounced around on floor, but for the most part, they stayed in my control. I reached inside and grabbed one—a brown one. I faltered before I popped it in my mouth. Here I'd been so excited about eating again, but now that the moment was upon me, the very thought of swallowing that piece of candy made me nauseous. It had been so long since my stomach had known food. Even now the muscle felt tight and bloated. How would it react? I'd probably become as sick as a dog. But it was the only thing on the menu.

My teeth bit into the candy shell. I chewed. My eyes closed in glorious ecstasy as my mouth inflamed with the flavors of chocolate and peanut, sugar and salt. Oh, heavens, it was good! And yet chewing felt so strange, so mechanical, as if my mind had forgotten how my jaw worked. Swallowing felt even more unnatural and I immediately craved water to wash it down. I grabbed an empty vitamin samples box, leaned out the door, and scooped up a supply of snow. Then I stuffed a handful of whiteness into my mouth and let it melt down my throat, washing the residue of chocolate flavor down with it.

I repeated this procedure again and again, eating the candy and then washing it down with a mouthful of snow. I fought the urge to fill my mouth with as many candies as it would hold—I did not want to get sick. I only wanted the energy. I couldn't afford to get sick. It was the day before Christmas Eve. And the day after tomorrow I had a place where I desperately wanted to be.

Despite my efforts, it was still hard to control the pace. I was eating too fast. After about ten pieces of the candy, I started to retch. I leaned my head out the door and sure enough, it all came up.

I pulled myself back inside and lay on the floor of the camper, reeling with frustration. *Please God!* I prayed again. *Let me keep it down. I have to keep it down!*

After a few minutes I tried again. I followed the same routine as before, only I did it slower. I chewed as long as I possibly could, grinding up every part of the peanut before I swallowed. A short time later I felt sick again. I lay out straight and refused to move a muscle. Somehow, I managed to keep it down. I waited for at least an hour before eating any more. My stomach growled incessantly as it tried to figure out what to do with this new and unusual substance called food.

Finally, I felt well enough to start again. But I also felt something else. The sugar and carbohydrates in that food were filtering into every part of my body like a warm drip from a life-saving IV. The feeling was spreading fast. It was incredible. My focus was clearing. My mind seemed to be clearing as well. I was able to dream about the future. I could see myself holding my beautiful wife and children on a sunlit day in some remote, warm, tropical place. We would be laughing and crying. A real eternal family.

And yet it was still so far from reality. I was really no closer to getting out of here now than I had been thirteen days ago. Even as I continued to consume the candy in the same methodical, disciplined manner, I knew there was no way that I could hope to restore the energy that I'd felt before this ordeal began. But there was another kind of energy that seemed to be filling the deficit. The energy of life itself. The power of my God, and the power of my living choice.

THURSDAY, DECEMBER 24

Day 14

The car was very quiet. The radio played the tunes of Christmas, but the volume was very low. Tonight was Christmas Eve. It was Christmas Eve . . .

We turned west at a little town called Belfry and made our way down a narrow highway through the weathered remains of some old mining platforms, collapsing under the weight of years. Nearly all the flyers were gone now. Only a handful lay in Tamara's lap. Corban, bless his heart, had fallen asleep on Zackary's shoulder. For the first time in a long time his older brother made no effort to push him aside. In fact, he seemed comforted by Corban's presence.

The mood was somber and grim. Tomorrow was Christmas. Despite all that I had said about not getting their hopes up, they'd allowed them to rise just the same. How could they have helped it? They'd wanted so badly to find him before Christmas, or at least learn some clue to help us to solve the mystery. Coming to Montana now seemed like a mistake. We'd come because it gave us a sense of empowerment, not waiting for fate. Our feelings of help-

lessness now seemed heavier than they otherwise might have been.

No, *I told myself. It had been worth it. Just to feel that sacred faith and strength for a day or a few hours—I wouldn't have traded it for anything.* I must still love him, *I concluded. I wondered if I loved him more than I ever had. Given the choice, I was sure I'd have made this trip all over again. I'd have made it a hundred times.*

I knew there were cases—I'd seen them portrayed on television—cases where the missing father or husband or child was never seen again. Their families were left forever with an empty place in their hearts, pondering the mystery to the end of their days, never knowing if their loved one had been killed, or kidnapped, or if they had simply run away.

As I pictured myself the newest member of that terrible affiliation, my heart knotted up with pain. There had to be something I was missing. Something I was overlooking. Perhaps that's why I'd taken that turn at Belfry. The prayers in my heart had never ceased, and something told me that I needed to see that final stretch of highway leading to Yellowstone Park—the one that the policeman said was closed.

We reached a town called Red Lodge and turned left toward the mountains at the first juncture. I saw the flashing sign proclaiming that the Beartooth Highway was closed for the season, but I drove past it anyway.

"Where are you going, Mom?" Tamara asked. "We passed three motels and a gas station. We still have a few more flyers."

"In a minute," I said. "I just want to see something . . ." My voice drifted off.

We wound our way up the rocky canyon alongside an ice-crusted stream and past snow-caked pine trees. The road was covered with a dangerous layer of packed ice. My tires slipped a bit at one of the corners. Corban awakened. Everyone became fully alert.

"Slow down, Mom," said Zack. "What are you looking for?"

"I—I don't know," I said awkwardly. "I just wanted to see how far it goes."

I found out a mile further. A gate suddenly appeared in front of us, crossing both lanes of the highway. I stopped the car just a few feet away. Beyond the barricade the road had a layer of snow at least three feet deep. I climbed out of the car.

"Where are you going?" asked Corban.

"Nowhere," I replied.

I stepped up to the gate and wrapped my fingers around the cold, silver padlock that bolted it shut. Then I stared off into the high mountain wilderness beyond and felt an icy shiver work its way up my back. My children had joined me. They were looking up at me strangely.

"What's the matter, Mom?" asked Zackary.

I stared off for another few seconds, then I turned to my son, feeling a little foolish.

"Nothing," I said. "Come on. It's cold. Let's get back in the car."

As we made our way back down the winding canyon road toward the town of Red Lodge, Tamara noticed that my cheeks were streaked with tears.

"Are you all right?" she asked.

"Yes," I replied, wiping both eyes hastily with the back of my hand. "It's nothing. Let's put up the rest of those flyers."

I saw that we also needed gas. There was an Amoco station up ahead. I turned in and rolled up to the fuel pump. As I prepared to fill up the car with Unleaded, Tamara took one of the flyers and walked inside. Through the window I saw her show Ben's picture to the attendant, a rather wiry-looking man wearing a baseball cap.

* * *

I didn't leave on the day I found the candy. By the time I'd finished consuming that first bag of M&Ms, it was already late afternoon. Shortly it would have been dark. I wish to God I hadn't waited. That last night had been full of stars and a bright, clear sky. I would have seen the light, that beacon in the distance, as clearly as a lighthouse. It would have been like setting out on my own Christmas pilgrimage, following the holy star in the night sky to that manger in Bethlehem, the place of salvation.

By morning, to my astonishment, virtually all of the energy I'd felt the night before had dissipated. I'd slept it off. And all I had left was a couple handfuls of candy, just the amount that had been inside the actual dispenser. It was from this stash that I expected to gather enough strength to reach that beacon.

Soon after eating a few more pieces, the buzz of energy returned, filling every vein and capillary with a kind of living electricity. Before departing, I located another of my children's presents in the closet—the package containing the pocketknife for my oldest son.

After tearing it open, I stuck the knife in my jacket. Then I drew in a deep breath for courage, and opened the rear door of the camper.

I pushed through the deep snow toward a cluster of pine trees to the west. I was leaving the security of my pickup for the very last time. But the sun was bright and the air was warm. I was sure it was a good omen. A magnificent omen. Nothing could stop me from reaching my family.

As soon as I arrived at the trees, I began cutting pine boughs and tying them together with twine. My aim was to construct a pair of snowshoes in the same manner as the ones manufactured by Weymouth. I may not have been a modern frontiersman like ol' Weymouth, but when I had finished the task a couple hours later, I was rather proud of my work and proceeded to tie the contraptions to the bottoms of my feet.

Only as I finished the last knot and stood up straight to see the landscape ahead did I experience the day's first spell of delirium. My labors had exhausted me more than I had expected. I fought hard to keep my balance and hastily consumed another dozen pieces of candy. By now my food supply for the entire day was half gone, and I hadn't even begun the actual trek.

But at last the moment of departure had arrived. So with another walking stick filling my hands and an indomitable determination burning in my guts, I set out toward the southwest and the landmarks of white-shrouded granite that I had judged to be exactly in line with the beacon of light.

I walked at a steady pace, not too fast or slow, trying to maintain a specific rhythm. I'd been at it for about two and a half hours when the clouds moved over me and shut out the light of the sun. It was like the closing of a curtain. Nevertheless, I kept on. The afternoon started waning late. I was amazed at how fast the day had gone. By my estimates, I'd only traveled about two or three miles across the endless snow plain. I must have looked like an insect on a vast wrinkled bedsheet, pursued only by a trail of tracks.

My success thus far had been attributed to eating a certain amount of candy at very specific intervals. It was like fuel—fuel with a very precise mileage of twenty to thirty yards. At last came the moment when I reached into my pocket and found nothing at all. At first I thought it was an error. My eyes darted around, half-wondering if I'd been robbed, or if I'd torn a hole in my jacket. But there was no robbery and no hole. The fuel was gone. My engines were starting to sputter. I couldn't believe it! I'd looked upon those little M&Ms almost as magic pellets, a kind of ambrosia from the gods that would have sustained me to any destination. I realized now that I'd wasted far too much time making the snowshoes.

The wind started to gust, and specks of ice began stinging my face. Nevertheless, my determination became more powerful than ever. This had become much more than a test of endurance. It now represented something far greater. A test of devotion. A test for the weeks and months and years. A test for eternity.

Toward evening, a grueling atrophy started to settle into my muscles. I felt like I was walking through a bog of mud. My steps were only a third as long as they had been. Still, I continued to prod myself onward, maintaining my faith that in the end, I would still be victorious.

Nature turned on the wind machines even harder. A powerful gust actually blew me off balance. I became tripped up in my snowshoes and went down. One of the snowshoes was torn right off my heel. I tried to tie it back on, my fingers numbing in the cold, but the thing had simply fallen apart. There was no way of repairing it. I looked around. There were no trees to construct a new one for miles in any direction.

The sun was starting to set. I gazed off toward the horizon line to the southwest. My heart fluttered. I could see a distinct glow. The mystery light! It was brighter than ever. I was so close! I couldn't give up now. I'd worked too hard, come too far.

With my jaw clenched like steel and my eyes full of icy tears, I struggled to my feet and fought my way through the drifts on one snowshoe. One of my legs sank deep with every step. I tried to compensate by pushing off with my other leg and hoisting myself forward. Just a few more yards, I told myself. A few more yards and I would be at the top of a rise. From there I felt certain I would be able to see into some sort of valley. At the bottom would lie the source of that glow. I was sure of it. I needed to see that light source. Just the sight of it would be enough to give me the final impetus to go on.

I fought harder. One more step! That's all I needed. The snow became too deep. Instead of making that final step, I simply fell forward. I dropped to my hands and knees, focusing my eyes straight ahead.

It was just enough. I could barely see over the top.

But the sight froze the blood as it surged through my heart. My mind plunged into desolation.

There was indeed a light. But it was clear now that it was at least another three or four miles in the distance. It might have been a cabin. It might have been some sort of survey tower for the Forest Service. But nothing could change the fact that between me and this light lay an impassable gulf with cliffs and ravines and ice-covered lakes, the details of which were being overtaken by the shadow of the setting sun. I couldn't understand it. I'd fought so hard. Was this it? Had I been beaten? I lowered my head. It was just too far.

Suddenly I raised my gaze. Blazing yellow eyes appeared from the other side of the rise, flying at me like headlights. I realized my oversight at once. How could I have failed to anticipate the enemy, the predator of my soul? I felt sure the creature had been there all along, crouching just beyond my view, waiting until the moment when I was most vulnerable, like always.

I gasped. The menacing hulk slammed into my chest and threw me backwards. Terror split my heart. But the terror was short-lived. My whole frame erupted into a mindless fury. Even as we landed in an explosion of snow and the wolf dug its teeth into my shoulder, I was groping for my son's knife in my pocket. If I was going to die, this demon, this wraith, was going to die with me.

Its jaws ripped away the material on my shoulder and made a lash at my face. Somehow I'd kept my grip on the walking stick. I thrust it into the wolf's head and managed to roll away. The knife was in my left hand now. I abandoned the stick to try and open the blade.

The beast landed on my back, smashing me flat. I nearly lost my hold on the knife. Its teeth latched onto my collar. Its claws caught my ear as well, but the cartilage was already so numb with frostbite that I didn't feel it. The wolf started dragging me, trying to turn me over to get a better angle on my throat. It took every ounce of my concentration to pull that blade out of its groove.

At last I'd done it! The knife locked into place just as the beast released my collar and made a lunge at my face. I thrust my fist upward. The knife found its mark in the beast's neck. I felt its warm blood on my hand. But the creature did not yelp. It struck back, digging its teeth into my forearm.

The wolf wrenched my arm backwards. I heard the bone snap. The limb went immobile as I felt a lightning bolt of pain. It had broken my arm! I cried out in agony and dropped the knife in the snow. The wolf released my disabled limb and moved in for the kill. I flopped over on my side in a feeble effort to protect my throat, and moved my left arm under my chest to support my weight.

I felt the hard round metal of the knife handle under my elbow. My fingers snatched it up just as the wolf's fangs came down on the soft flesh of my neck. I stabbed upward, sinking the knife deep between the animal's ribs. The sound I heard was not a gasp. Not a yelp. It was more like an exhale, cut mercifully short. Its jaws went limp a mere instant before it would have torn out my jugular. The wolf collapsed onto my chest and lay there, still and warm. Not even a final breath. Not even a last convulsion. It was simply dead. Stabbed through the heart, or so I surmised. I wouldn't have thought any wound could kill something so quickly. It was as if someone had thrown a switch. Its power source had been cut. The game was over.

With my uninjured arm I heaved the carcass off my chest and rolled onto my belly. I tried to rise, but my left arm wasn't strong enough to push me to my feet. My right arm hung uselessly at my side. Tears of frustration melted into the snow. I started to crawl, my good arm pushing me along. I made it several yards. I made it several more. I fought for another inch. At last I could go no further. I rolled onto my back, my lungs heaving for breath.

The ordeal was over. I'd beaten the lupus, but it had also beaten me. I'd done all I could. It just wasn't enough. I released an awful cry into the storm. Then all went quiet. The wind itself became a distant echo.

With my last ebb of strength, I reached into my pocket and pulled out the box containing the sapphire necklace, my peace offering for Jillian. I held it to my chest, the tears freezing to my cheeks. There was nothing left for me now. Nothing but to let the winds and snows cover me over like a blanket, and die.

So that's my story.

I've told it from the heart. I've told it from the depths of my fading consciousness, though only the winds and the snows and the lonely Beartooth Mountains will ever know it.

But despite my failure, despite all my pain and regret, all is well enough now. Amazingly, I feel an incredible sense of peace. It flows inside me like the easy current of a listless stream. That's something I hadn't expected. I'd expected to feel only tremendous agony at this moment, the moment of my death. But I guess Heavenly Father has decided I've had enough. And as evidence of His good will, He has sent down to me from the eternal realms the final emblem of His mercy—an angel of light. She's arriving just now, and I am blinded by the brightness of her smile.

So it appears I'll be spending my last Christmas with God. And every Christmas thereafter. Only a short time ago this prospect would have filled me with devastating regret. Now it fills me with trembling expectation. After all, He *is* Christmas. He *made* Christmas. Who would not want to spend Christmas with its Author? Who wouldn't willingly wait for hours in the pressing crowd just to catch of glimpse of His sleeping face in the Bethlehem manger? Or make the long journey to kneel at His side in the garden or under the cross? It's clear to me now, the lessons that a hundred relentless teachers tried to pound into my brain. He is the Gift Giver, the Prince of Peace, the Greatest who made Himself the Least, the Servant who paid the price for our souls. Who would not want to feel forever the love that I feel now in the resplendence of immortality?

I only regret that it took so long for me to understand. I guess I'm a little slower than most. I'm not sure what I could have done to learn it any sooner. And in light of all that's happened, perhaps this was always His point.

I pray that God will watch over my family. My little ones, my Jillian. Though I may never tell her the things I had to say or hold my children in my arms on

Christmas morning, perhaps as they gather around the tree, their faces aglow with the thousands of multi-colored lights, a portion of my love may be gathered with them, warming the room and warming their hearts.

I have to close my eyes now. I can no longer hold them open. I'll just keep them shut until the angel takes my hand in her own. Or maybe I won't open them at all until I've arrived at my Savior's side in the bosom of paradise.

And perhaps then I might ask Him, if the time is right, how it is that the descent of an angel sounds so much like the rotary blades of a helicopter.

WHAT I DID FOR CHRISTMAS

A Third-Grade Essay
By
Corban Wylie

I had a really great Christmas this year. In fact it was my best Christmas ever.

I spent it in Montana which may seem kind of funny because I've never been to Montana before. Me and my mom and my brother, Zackary, and my sister, Tamara, all got in the car and drove there a few days before Christmas. We were looking for my dad. He was missing and we were all really worried. So when the police couldn't find him, we decided we had better go and look for him ourselves.

We drove to a city called Billings. We showed his picture to a lot of different people who worked in gas stations and motels and places like that. It was hard at first because nobody had seen him. But then my sister showed his picture to a man at a gas station in a town called Red Lodge. The man said he had seen my dad a few weeks before. He said it was on the day right before a very big storm. He said my dad told him that he was driving up over a mountain called Beartooth.

My mom got real nervous and went back to the police and got a whole bunch of people to help us, including a man with a helicopter who worked for Search and Rescue. This man flew up over the mountain with some other men and found my dad's pickup buried in the snow. He said he wouldn't have found it at all except he saw some footprints going away from it. He tried to follow the footprints with his helicopter, but it was getting dark and the wind was getting bad so he wasn't sure if he should keep looking or go home. I'm very glad that he kept looking because he found my dad on the top of a mountain. My dad was almost frozen solid through, but the man rescued him and brought him to the hospital.

I was so happy when I saw my dad. He is my hero. We were all so, so, very, very, happy and cried a lot. My mom cried too. We spent Christmas in the hospital with my dad. They warmed him up really good and gave him liquid food to eat and put his arm in a cast.

My dad said he broke his arm fighting a wolf. I asked the man who flew the helicopter if he saw the wolf that my dad had killed but he said there was no wolf. He told my mom that my dad was very sick and may have been seeing things. But I told him if my dad said he saw a wolf then he saw a wolf and after that the man smiled and said it was okay for me to think that.

In the hospital my dad told us that he loved us very much. He hugged Zackary and told him he was sorry for all the time they had missed doing stuff together and that he would be there for him from now on. He told Tamara that too and kissed her. Then he hugged me and said we would do a lot of fun things together when he got better. I love my dad so much. I never wanted to let him go.

After that my dad held my mom's hands and gave her a necklace with a pretty blue stone shaped like a dove. He told her that he loved her too and that he was sorry. My mom started to cry. My dad said he wanted for us to try again to be a family again. My mom didn't look like she knew what to say at first. My dad said he knew it was going to take some time, but that he was willing to take all the time in the world.

I didn't get that many presents this year, partly because my dad said he ate one of my presents. But I didn't care. I just wanted my dad and that's what I got and I didn't want anything else. And next year if I have to write about what I did for Christmas again, I hope I don't have that much of an exciting story to tell like this year. I hope all that I have to tell is that we were all of us together and that we were a family.

Because that's what matters the most. And that's what I've learned this Christmas. And it's the best lesson that I think anybody could ever, ever, ever, ever, learn.

PHOTO BY "PICTURE THIS... by Sara Staker"

ABOUT THE AUTHOR

A Light in the Storm is the twelfth novel that Chris has written in a period of just as many years, thrilling audiences with his wide-ranging grasp of numerous storytelling genres including fantasy adventure *(Tennis Shoes Adventure Series)*, science fiction *(Eddie Fantastic)*, historical *(Daniel and Nephi)*, and contemporary *(A Return to Christmas)*, all the while striving to celebrate LDS heritage and values. Chris says, "One of the goals of my life is to show aspiring Mormon artists—and artists throughout the world—that great stories can be told that reach deeply into our souls without compromising one single spark of that immortal fire that defines us as Christians.

With *A Light in the Storm*, Chris has attempted to take his storytelling to a new level. According to Chris, *"A Light in the Storm,* though not as long as some of my other books, is by far the most difficult book I have ever written; with more drafts, more crumpled paper, and more trips back to the drawing board than any of my other projects. Only when I realized—with the help of my eternal companion, Beth—that the story of Ben Wylie is, in many ways, my *own* story, and that looking into his soul was like looking into a mirror, did the project truly begin to breathe life. I hope others out there can see themselves in that same mirror, before they've lost something of infinite importance."

Chris resides in Riverton, Utah, with his wife, Catherine Elizabeth, and their three children, Steven Teancum, Christopher Ammon, and Alyssa Sariah. Visit Chris' adventurous Web site at **www.cheimerdinger.com**, and become a registered guest.